W9-BQZ-450

THE ATLAS OF REDS AND BLUES

The Atlas

of

Reds and Blues

A NOVEL

Devi S. Laskar

COUNTERPOINT
BERKELEY, CALIFORNIA

THE ATLAS OF REDS AND BLUES

Although *The Atlas of Reds and Blues* is inspired by actual events and
people, it is a work of fiction. Many of the events portrayed here actually
took place, but the author's rendering of those events and their particulars
are invented. The characters' thoughts, conversations, and actions
are a work of imagination.

Grateful acknowledgment for reprinting materials
is made to the following:

Vandana Khanna, "Blackwater Fever" from *Train to Agra*.
Copyright © 2001 by Vandana Khanna. Reprinted by permission
of Southern Illinois University Press.

Library of Congress Cataloging-in-Publication Data
Names: Laskar, Devi S., author.
Title: The atlas of reds and blues : a novel / Devi S. Laskar.
Description: First hardcover edition. | Berkeley, California :
    Counterpoint, 2019.
Identifiers: LCCN 2018023436 | ISBN 9781640091535
Classification: LCC PS3612.A846 A95 2019 | DDC 813/.6—dc23
LC record available at https://lccn.loc.gov/2018023436

Jacket design by Nicole Caputo
Book design by Wah-Ming Chang

COUNTERPOINT
2560 Ninth Street, Suite 318
Berkeley, CA 94710
www.counterpointpress.com

Printed in the United States of America
Distributed by Publishers Group West

1 3 5 7 9 10 8 6 4 2

For
Anjini, Ellora, Devrani

&

For
Joy

with all the light left in the world

I could trace it like a geography of
someone I had once been

VANDANA KHANNA

THE ATLAS OF REDS AND BLUES

TROUBLE SWALLOWING

Now this fainting, this falling, this landing so ungainly. Concrete scratches her face, the back of her arm. Her legs twist like licorice.

Nearby, it sounds like cocktail hour at a convention of common starlings: a murmur punctuated by intermittent laughter. Why? The sky marbles blue and white, but the clouds are leaving town. She closes her eyes, breathes in the metal essence of her own blood as it exits the hole the bullet has created.

The last time she smelled this iron: 1997. Blood on the toilet seat, blood on the tile, guilt flooding like ocean water overhead. She shouldn't have gone home that day after her collapse. She should have driven herself to the hospital. Maybe that baby could have been saved. Still, that was thirteen years ago. Three babies since then, alive and thriving, but she's at once on the driveway and back in the employee bathroom, washing that blood off the long-since-discarded skirt in the white sink, wiping away the blood on her fingertips with brown paper towels.

Her eyelids so heavy now but she possesses the power of flight. Her spine against the concrete of the driveway, cold, but her mind the jumble and rattle of a projector running continuously, a moving picture made of stills, but not a silent movie, a kaleidoscope of time and place, an atlas of the past. The call of other voices: husband's, children's, sister's, and the sharp bark of Greta, the shepherd who's been dead for almost two years, of a degenerative disease. Other voices too, unfamiliar, newly introduced, the policemen and their dispatchers; and voices of those so dear but gone long before the babies came. Her eyelids so heavy. How much liquid has spilled near the heart, toward the stomach? Why is the act of spilling liquid so painful? Suddenly realizing: this is a miscarriage of a different kind.

No baby to lose this time.

A different kind of secession.

The owl that has been living in the tree outside the bedroom window hoots to the agent's assault-rifle trigger call. She—daughter, wife, and mother of three—tries to open eyes, mouth. Film ends. Light shining on blank screen, screen dissolving into page, something she can read. Pain shifts. An outline. Not a chalk outline, or the outline of a body for the shooters at the practice range. But Aristotle's Incline, an outline of a story, an explanation of why her back is to the concrete. Every story has a beginning, a middle, an end. Aristotle's ski-lift structure with seven stops, outlined in his *Poetics*, a book she has studied and restudied over the years. She begins searching for the words that will form her beginning; that will anchor the story, her own story, in its ordinary world. She reads the words that form as she remembers . . .

MOVING DAY IN THE

ORDINARY WORLD

. . . In which she moves thirteen long miles to a new house, three girls in tow, their beloved shepherd parked in a kennel, their belongings painstakingly packed box by box and hauled over from the old house bit by bit, the man of the hour, her husband, on a business trip, first France and then Japan, during this entire event. They move from the boundaries of Atlanta's city limits to just inside the enclosing arms of suburbia. Black clouds waste no time: heavens open up, trees swing like pendulums, thunder fails to cease. The rain unrelenting, impassable roads under perpetual construction, strip malls decorated in neon, gated brick monstrosities and carpet-soft lawns, ravines covered in kudzu, etched metal historical markers dot streets like stop signs—subtly cele-

brating the Confederacy one hundred and thirty-nine years
after the loss; commuters honking a concerto of road rage,
the smog-laced air they all breathe, and a pair of shopgirls
crossing the street when they see her coming . . .

&

She's a chronicler of the dead. Obituaries. A lowly job, usually given to interns first, those who are new to the newspaper world; or those old-timers who could not stomach
the deadlines or the politics of daily journalism; those who
could not stand the constant criticism from the public. For
the first time in ten years, since the year 2000, Mother arrives last to her section of the newsroom, far from the windows that look out to the skyscrapers crowding the urban
landscape, the street way below, downtown Atlanta. Editor
Dennis on the phone. His face is red and crumpled like used
gift wrap. Dennis does not wave. He swivels his chair back
to his computer screen as though he doesn't see her. Her
other two colleagues are absent, rather their things, lunch
bags, jackets, notebooks, are dumped over their desk cal-
endars, but their bodies are not present. She looks around
and there are reporters in the thick of the newsroom where
the City Desk journalists cluster, crowding around the wa-
tercooler, watching live TV on multiple screens. She grips
the jangle of keys in her left hand. Where is the car parked?
What route had she taken this morning after a breakfast of
toaster strudel and black tea?

    She is achy, content to sit. Desk is tidy. Facing the nar-
row corridor that leads to the restrooms. Desk is tidy because there is no work to carry over, day to day. At workday's
end, she files the notes and the notebook into the cavernous

drawers, touches the four-by-six color photo of her family tacked onto the bulletin board, and rushes home. Today no lunch and no jacket, not even a purse. Why? No one looks at her, no one gives her anything to do.

She used to be a crime reporter, used to have to keep watch over everything that had to do with her assigned police municipalities, the courthouses in the counties she covered. She practices still; who goes in and out of the corridor and the bathrooms, how many times each day. Who goes in, who doesn't come out. Who goes in pensive and comes out giddy. Who goes in all nervous energy and comes out sated, slow. She gleans George the metro police reporter's coke habit this way, and the fact that the assistant food editor, Julie, has been having an affair with Charles, the morning editor at the City Desk, for three months. How do they have the time? They are each married, and have kids on the same Little League team. Car pool must have become a hotbed of innuendo and long looks.

She turns back to Dennis, but he is occupied by the urgent call on the telephone. His sweat and the anger rolling off his back build an ill wind.

Now she is neither an intern nor a shadow. She is a seasoned reporter with a husband who knows which kiosk sells the best croissants at Charles de Gaulle Airport better than he knows where the cough medicine is stored at home. She is a mother of three small children. A woman who does not want to let go of her former life, a woman who cannot stand the mind-numbing repetition of her present. Once the children came in quick succession, she accepted this job, writing about the accomplishments and attributes of a person who will never read the work and tell her that she got it wrong.

Today, no file resting atop the desk calendar. She longs to swivel the chair three hundred and sixty degrees, like the children do when they visit her workplace on occasion. She longs to scrounge the desk for loose change, see what could be had from the vending machines for lunch. But she scrounged last Tuesday, and for those efforts ate chocolate-covered peanuts, the candy coating smudging her files. So there's no change to be had. She could ask to borrow a few dollars, but doesn't want to ask. She can't remember exactly when she last spied her purse or her jacket. She doesn't want to be imprecise, especially at work. Position tenuous and part-time. If there is a bloodletting, cutbacks, she will be the first to be let go.

The number of reporters watching TV balloons. Their collective undertone sounds like bees surrounding a hive. She sighs. It sounds like the hive of bees making a home in the tree in her backyard. The keys bunched in her left hand bloom into a metallic sprig. An owl hoots on the TV, and then she knows why they are watching. They are watching the spectacle at her house. They are watching her through the magic of television.

Dennis yells, "God damn it!" and hangs up the telephone. His face almost purple. He rises from his chair, looks through her. Because she is really not there, she is on her driveway bleeding. He staggers to the men's room. Goosebumps cover her arms and her head begins to ache at the temples. The timer on her phone buzzes insistently in her right hand, but she doesn't turn it off. Can't remember how. The phone rings. The number scrolls across the top of her screen. She gets up and dashes to the elevator. Immediately, she's back at the car. A few moments later she's navigating the toll road, the goodbyes to the children this morning echoing. And then a second later, she's in her driveway again, prostrate, pain expanding at the rate of the universe, and men crawling like ants, searching her car.

&

The tired adage holds some truth in its scaffold: they are never meant to be heard. Like children, most dolls are made only to be seen, put on display. Real live dolls are taught to remain stoic, bear witness in silence, no matter how the consumer judges. The radio dispatcher squawks and a policeman's voice describes her: Black hair. Brown skin. Gray sweatpants. Brown T-shirt. Flip-flops.

The dispatcher's voice drawls. "Is she Black?"

A lawn mower sputters to life nearby and drowns out the policeman's reply.

Third Monday of May 2010. When you put American clothes on a brown-skinned doll, what do people see? The clothes? Or the whole doll? Or only the skin?

&

The baby doll arrives in a pink cardboard box, a toy with black hair and brown eyes, and skin like caramel crème. A gift presented from their paternal uncle, for the Real Thing (who will grow up to become Mother on the driveway) and the Baby Sister (who will grow up to become a nun). The girls' mother braids the baby doll's hair into a tiny plait. The Real Thing and the Baby Sister and the toy baby doll now match. Three dolls in small-town North Carolina. Their mother shakes her head every time the Real Thing or the Baby Sister cry. Their mother points to the doll: "See? She's a tough cookie. We never hear her cry." This refrain often repeats, no matter if the Real Thing and the Baby Sister don't want to eat lunch at the appointed hour, don't want to go to bed before the sun finishes setting, don't want to stop reading the book aloud. Out of the three of them, the toy baby doll never talks back, always closes her eyes when she is put down for a nap, never complains when their mother takes a kitchen rag and wipes the smudges of dirt from her face.

The toy baby doll is shoved into the black Samsonite rectangle the summer before she, the Real Thing, turns ten. The toy doll rides in the belly of the plane across the International Date Line in a suitcase-coffin and is bequeathed to a girl cousin in a crowded, noisy suburb of Calcutta. There is talk in the next room, where the maternal uncles sit and drink chai, about the Americans landing a probe on Mars the previous day. The Bengali grandmothers and great-aunts smooth their own hair with worn hands, the colored bangles on their arms tinkling like wind chimes heralding the start of a new day.

&

Their amusement echoes down the throat of the neighbor-hood, gathering volume as it reaches the cul-de-sac, the dead-end lung. The neighbors are dressed in tennis whites, their bottled-blond hair in ponytails. She can hear these real Barbie dolls, each stationed at the tops of their own drive-ways, watching and laughing, but what she pictures again is a murmuration of feathery starlings cresting and dipping in unison against the swath of sky.

&

Scratches scar the arms and legs of the pair of Barbie dolls their mother picks up from the consignment shop in Carrboro—as if the dolls' previous owner was trying to pierce the plastic skin to see what lay underneath. Their mother plucks miniature accessories from the curb, when the mean older girl across the street throws a fit loud enough for the entire neighborhood to hear and tosses all of her toys outside in a cardboard box. A hot-pink shoe and a blue one, and a pair of white sandals with frayed straps, a Barbie "bed" that is no better than a plastic gurney, one pastel pink skirt, and one orange-and-black top. The Real Thing and the Baby Sister empty out five shoeboxes storing old letters, buttons from coats long donated, paper clips, and use their stapler to fashion a "house," each room a diorama made from repurposed juice cans, padded manila envelopes, socks too holey to be darned. Their mother collects scraps from the material for aprons she sews in front of the TV most weekend evenings, and donates them to the Barbie improvement project. They watch the ads for a new movie, *Star Wars: Episode IV,* but their mother will not let them go, declaring it to be witchcraft and a waste of money. The Real Thing and the Baby Sister grow tired of the not entirely new perky Barbie dolls and their forced smiles and their scarred bodies. It is not *The Sound of Music* with Maria making play clothes from drapes for the Captain's seven children.

The Baby Sister strips the scraps from the Barbie girls and she, the Real Thing, fashions temporary transportation from the shoebox that was the Barbie sitting room in the cardboard dollhouse. "They have a better chance of getting new homes if they don't have ugly clothes," the Baby Sister says.

"They have a better chance if the white girls near the river never know we played with them," the Real Thing says.

She and the Baby Sister put the dolls into the box, sitting up, side by side, and set them free down the tributary that leads to the Cape Fear River Basin some miles away. They wave goodbye and watch the box sail calmly downstream. Later, their mother says nothing as the Real Thing and the Baby Sister take the Barbie clothes and shoes and throw them in the trash.

&

Someone trips the switch for the red bullhorn on the squad car parked at the far end of the driveway, next to the blue recycling bin and green yard-waste container. "Good lord!" a voice exclaims. "Why does everything have to be so complicated?"

Mother is forty-three years, six months, and twenty-five days old.

&

Today, the Middle Daughter gets in Mother's car after school—in tears, sobbing that her new classmate won't invite her home. "Annette said her mom won't let her play with Black people outside of school." Middle Daughter's shoulders slump forward in her seat. Everyone in the first grade is invited to the special premiere of *Bee Movie* at the Buckhead mansion of Annette's famous athlete uncle—everyone but her.

Mother drives back to school, leaves the car idling in the fire lane, and marches into the office. "Why are children allowed to even say such trash?" The teachers and administration look as blank as stretched canvas. "You know they are hearing this from their families." The school employees simply fix their eyes on a point just past her shoulder and stare. "What are you going to do?" Their silence is the loudest thing she's ever heard.

She marches back to the car, a wooden soldier on fire, plotting.

"Don't tell Daddy," Middle Daughter says to Mother as soon as she straps on the seat belt.

That girl has always been able to read her mother's face like a road map. "Why not?"

"He'll be sad, and he has to go out of town for work."

"So what? He needs to know." She pauses, eyes the last piece of cinnamon-flavored gum in the cup holder but leaves it. "Besides, he's already out of town for work."

Middle Daughter is shaking her head. "No, he'll be sad."

Mother is hardly out of the pristine neighborhood that surrounds the school when the patrol car passes her, makes a smooth three-point turn, flashing red lights, deejaying a siren. "Stop the vehicle," the robotic voice booms through a bullhorn.

Mother pulls her car to the shoulder, whips out the registration and her license, rolls down the window. The policeman is young, the hair on his head a newly hatched chick, fuzzy, translucent blond. "Here you go," she says before he opens his mouth to speak.

He grunts. "You missed the yield." He bends his head and clocks first the passenger seat, her purse zipper open, a dog-eared copy of *One Hundred Years of Solitude* splayed, spine up; then the back row and Middle Daughter calmly eating a cereal bar and looking away, out her window to the wrought-iron gates and what stands on the other side: a water fountain, a rose garden, and a columned house. An American flag from the 1790s, thirteen stars in a circle, flaps proudly atop a flagpole; underneath it a Confederate flag, with its iconic Southern Cross, waves in the wind.

Mother does not argue that the sign has been absent, removed, for years now; that the hedges at that soft intersection have been trimmed back so that all parties can see one another. She does not argue that he has been stopping her regularly, usually in the mornings. She recognizes him, but he never recognizes her. For the first time, she fails to apologize.

His stride back to the car is deliberate and purposeful. He returns, a pink ticket in his hand. "Pay close attention," he says, his eyes as blue as a cloudless day. "Don't let me catch you here again."

She nods in agreement, though she knows she'll see him again within the next week and that he won't recognize her, and then rolls up her window. "Don't tell Daddy," she says.

Middle Daughter grins, then grimaces. Her eyes look down toward her hands. "Why not?"

"He'll be sad," she says.

&

The pain like an ambulance call, waxing and waning as the red light circles through a complete revolution.

&

She calls out for help. The blood pouring out of her is steady and strong; a river, not a monthly tributary. She is almost out of toilet tissue. She flushes the toilet again. She spies the bath towel but it will require her to stand up and take a few steps. "Something's wrong," she hollers. "I can't stop the bleeding."

But she pleads to deaf ears. She knows exactly what her husband is doing: he is wearing his headphones and listening to music and waiting for the timer to sound. Greta is outside chasing squirrels. When the timer sounds, he will unplug his headphones and call for their shepherd, their first baby, to come inside. Then he will call out for Greta's human mother, and tell her it's time to go to their friends' house for dinner. There will be exasperation in his voice when she doesn't answer, when she doesn't magically appear at the bottom of the stairs, ready to go. But then he will be curious, and will come looking for her. She knows it is close to the time they will have to leave. She turns her head to the left and sees the dress she was planning to wear to the party, white with tiny eyelet flowers stitched at the collar and the hem, cap sleeves. White is the color of mourning in her parents' world, in her parents' culture. How appropriate. She can wear white to the hospital instead, to confirm what she already knows: that the baby no bigger than a peanut that she's been wishing and worrying for, for nearly seven years, has left her. She looks at her hands, awash with blood that smells of iron and copper and steel. She will come home after the hospital and lie in her bed, her head propped up by pillows, a TV remote on the nightstand to change the channel. The TV will remain on for days and days, a steady chatter of talk shows and game shows and news to drown out the silence, the countdown clock ticking toward a due date that no longer matters.

&

The dispatcher's radio crackles. "Well, Hollis, at least you got to work on your hobby today."

The agent laughs hard. "Which one?"

The crackle repeats. "Both, I guess. You always do love to brandish your weapon while working on your tan."

Mother remembers the motorist in Alabama, being interviewed by PBS, right after the last election, his farmer's tan, his candy-red pickup brandishing a gun rack in the back—and a sticker of a skeleton draped in the Confederate flag. "I'm not racist," the motorist insisted to the blue-suited reporter holding a mic. "Don't tell my friends, but I voted blue for the first time."

The first American president with a permanent tan has been in office for sixty-eight weeks and six days.

&

Holly Hobbie dolls are sold out. Their mother fishes for substitutes out of the clearance bin at the Durham department store going-out-of-business sale. Two of them, actually. One for her, the Real Thing, and one for the Baby Sister. The rag babies carry painted smiles and blue eyes drawn to look down.

The pasty-faced cashier explains the meaning of *Buy one, get one free* at the checkout.

"Two for one price!" their mother exclaims, pulling the cash out of her red cloth handbag.

The new owners are not happy Holly Hobbie is unavailable. The new owners know the price of admission into any circle of friends at school or even in the neighborhood this year is the Holly Hobbie doll, with her patchwork quilt dress and blue bonnet and black Mary Jane shoes. The Baby Sister is quick to put her rag baby in the black Samsonite suitcase-coffin months before the next trip to see the cousins in India, but the Real Thing does not. She carefully keeps her doll atop her twin bed, propped into a sitting position by her well-loved pillow. She uses a blue rubber band to get the yellow yarn hair out of the doll's face. She cuts out a picture of the Holly Hobbie doll from the Sunday mailer that has the phrase "Sold Out" in red across the torso like a pageant sash—and croons to it the new song from *Grease* that's overtaken the radio airwaves: "You're the One That I Want."

&

The dispatcher's drawl echoes, too.

Never mind that she's been hearing this soliloquy from strangers since she was born, in the Year of the Fire Horse, twin sixes after the nineteen. Never mind the order of questions invariably changes even if the questions themselves do not: "How long have y'all lived here? Do you even speak English? Oh, well. Your English is so good. Bless your heart, you must miss your people. You stick out like a raisin in a big bowl of oatmeal. Is it true that you worship cows? Is it painful to have that red dot on your women's foreheads? Is that some bloody concoction? I learned about India when I was in grade school. Is it true y'all are all poor and beg in the street? If everybody's poor, where does the money come from? You certainly don't look hungry. Bless your heart, do you know about Weight Watchers? Do you worship idols? Bless your heart, that's akin to voodoo. I watched *Indiana Jones and the Temple of Doom*. I heard someone on TV say it was based on a true story. Do y'all really eat monkey brains? I'm so concerned for your soul. Have you considered accepting Jesus into your heart? I think it's funny you call your dress a sorry. I bet your mommas are sorry having to wear that contraption in public. How come y'all aren't laughing? Don't complain about my dog barking at you, and being off leash. You're in America now, you should do as the Romans do, go to Kmart down the street and buy yourself some pants. Right? You should be grateful. Fifty years ago I could have had you arrested just by the way you're looking at me right now. Maybe y'all should consider coming to our Bible study Wednesday night, it might do you some good. Have you even heard of the Bible? Don't get all uppity on me, don't turn away. I know you think you don't have to listen. But this is my country. You do. When are y'all heading back? Y'all best be getting back to where you came from, you hear? No need to overstay your welcome."

&

Two of the Kevlar-clad agents are within earshot.

"He's been picked up?" the first one asks, his voice raspy as if he'd smoked too many cigarettes.

"Ambush." The other voice chuckles. "He never saw it coming."

She remembers the birthday party for her hero the year before, all the stealth phone calls and e-mails, all the whispers between the girls. She remembers how surprised he'd been to see his oldest friends crowded around the candle-laden cake on the dining room table, singing off key. They'd parked half a mile away, so he wouldn't know as he drove home from his office that they were lying in wait. "Happy?" she'd asked.

"Perfect," he'd replied, his eyes shining with unshed tears.

&

She turns her eyes from the cloudy Cyclops looming across the satellite map of the Gulf of Mexico on the television screen, Hurricane Katrina bearing down on Louisiana in the coming day, to see her man of the hour dragging his scuffed shoes through the door. He walks into the kitchen, carry-on strap slung across his shoulder, hair tousled, the circles under his eyes like tree rings. He pets Greta and gives the girls bear hugs as they grab their backpacks and run out the door for the intermittent car pool she has managed to join. He stands there and she smells the weariness, the noxious airplane smell, on his clothes, on his skin.

He is home a day or two early.

She smiles and he smiles back. She knows that look in his bright blue eyes. He wants to have his day and spend it, too. He wants to sleep enough that he feels he's caught up on his rest but to wake in time to check his e-mail before it gets too late. He wants to go out for a run with his friends late enough that they have a chance to show up, but early enough that the overheated Southern sun doesn't bake their shadows along the trail. He wants to have someone squeeze some oranges in the juicer but he doesn't want to be that someone and he does not want to ask someone else to do it for him. It is almost eight o'clock in the morning and he is conflicted.

"Can I make you coffee?" he asks, then yawns. He runs

his hand through his dirty blond hair, starting to turn silver at the temples.

"My hero," she says, muting the TV with the blue button on the universal remote. She hugs him a second too long and he is the first to let go.

&

"Sounds like you really pushed that gal's button, Hollis."

The agent snorts. "People come into your life as a blessing or a lesson, Paula."

Laughter. "Which one are you, Hollis?"

&

It is just a game, a pastime they play to pass the time. Every footfall creates an expectant echo of guests who are not imminent—and the array of packing boxes has been breached. The Middle Daughter says, "Let's play the doctor game. I know where the doctor stuff is. I saw the injection thing in the bag that has the alphabet magnets."

The Eldest Daughter replies, "I hate playing that game. All we do is lie down. And you always want to be the hero, the doctor." She is the girl who loves mankind but has disdain for man. She is already as tall as her maternal grandmother.

"I don't want to be the doctor today," Middle says. "I want to be the broken person." She is the girl who is so wrapped up in the idea of inventing convenient intergalactic travel that she has forgotten mankind and man, except for when an individual or a group of them single her out because of her looks, which are a lot like her mother's at that age, curly mop of hair, diminutive in stature.

Mother picks up a Magic Marker, jots down the exchange on the back of the pink packing slip. Her cell phone buzzes: a message from her dearest college friend. "Snagged your handsome husband at Logan. We need a witness for the ceremony!" Mother laughs, mostly to herself, and types back CONGRATULATIONS. She's missing Jess and Maya's official tying of the knot in Massachusetts because she's got to work, and because someone has to be home with the girls.

"Well, I don't want to be the doctor either," Eldest says. "I want to be the credit card person."

The Youngest Daughter laughs in appreciation. She is the boy-crazy girl, the one who has already figured out how to manipulate man and conquer mankind. She is the startling beauty, the one who will have to get an unlisted telephone number when it's her turn to go to high school and all the boys will want to drive her home. Youngest says, "I want to be the doctor. I want to push all the buttons."

&

Every day is *Groundhog Day*, Bill Murray version: 2005, 2006, 2007, 2008. She remains cloudy about the lessons she's supposed to be learning at the small hands of her girls.

She comes home from the gas station, her tank is full, her credit card more burdened. The Eldest Daughter says, "You think this is bad?" pointing to the Youngest Daughter, who has just thrown red-orange crayons into the heating vent, heaped all shades of blue crayons into the VCR, and licked the cabinet doorknobs in the kitchen. No particular reason. "Just wait until she grows up."

&

On the driveway her thirst is primitive: she wants to taste
the blue palette of cold water, she wants to dispel the rancid
ketchup taste blooming in her mouth.

&

They've hidden her baggie of chocolate-covered espresso beans. These girls who did not care for the breakfast she got up early to make: scrambled eggs and grits, biscuits and gravy. Cheddar grated from an orange-yellow block of Tillamook she'd been saving. Hash browns with crispy edges, smothered in ketchup. These girls who fed Greta three extra breakfasts today under the table when they thought no one was watching. She searches under the couch cushions and in their toy chests and the baggie is nowhere to be found. She really must have five or six right now or she will descend into a deep sleep and not pick up the children from school. Come to think of it, they were rather hyper before school today, when her hero called from Phoenix, the Super Bowl festivities lingering as background noise. The girls were jittery and especially loud, unable to restrain themselves: hitting, spitting, hissing, laughing, crying at one another. She had to interrupt his stories about the Giants' win by raising her voice, and commanding the girls to drink extra water, get ready for car pool. She had to let go of the call when they didn't listen, when the Youngest Daughter stuck out her tongue and the Eldest said she was the meanest mother ever, when the Middle slammed the door to the bathroom so hard the house shook.

She begins to understand why certain types of the clown fish species eat their young: the ingratitude, the ingratitude.

&

She imagines how this must look to the alien observer who has arrived from outer space: the life-size neighbor Barbie dolls maintaining their Southern hospitality smiles as they pick at imaginary lint on their tennis skirts, as they do a quick runway strut to the curb and look inside their mailboxes though the mailman will not arrive for several hours, as they initiate small talk about the golf pro at the country club.

Their applause ricochets down the cul-de-sac, and startles her. The neighbors' claps, ostensibly in delight, sound like fireworks. She cannot think of a single time when her own mother encouraged her to laugh at another person's misfortune. She cannot recall a single moment when her hero's mother did not stop and offer assistance to someone in distress.

One woman calls out in a syrupy accent, "Is that CNN pulling up?"

&

Once upon a time before children, she and her hero visited the Barbie museum in Japan. They learned the first Barbie dolls were born there in 1959, but the dolls themselves were white girls, either blonde or brunette, sporting a zebra-pattern one-piece bathing suit. At that time, Japanese housewives hand-stitched the limited number of outfits.

By 2004, Barbie was still a white girl, but she had "companions": siblings, a boyfriend, "friend" dolls from as far away as India. African American Barbie dolls were available too, but at a higher price. As well as hundreds of choices, mostly in clothes, but also in cars, homes, men named Ken.

By 2009, Barbie dolls had a clothing line that rivaled Prada, articles written about them in *Forbes* magazine, a marketing and design team in El Segundo, California, and a "store to playroom door" strategic team in Hong Kong.

&

The sun shines without pity but she shivers on the concrete. This will make a good book someday. The feeling in her legs starts to wane.

And a good movie. Brad Pitt can play the part of her hero. He loves Brad Pitt.

But she's too dark to be played by Angelina Jolie.

&

She wants to finish the novel she's been writing, sentence by sentence, comma by comma, since the girls were born. It is about a woman who does as she pleases, feels no remorse for wanting everything, feels no guilt for having some material possessions, feels no shame in her desire for equity and for her ambitions, climbs the corporate ladder with the same ease and muscle memory as a French chef concocting a soufflé, has love affairs, cures hunger and poverty, speaks her mind without consequence. It is a fairy tale that does not require a prince.

She opens her friend Emily's copy of Aristotle's *Poetics*, sees the handwritten note addressed to her on the title page: "Look at the incline, how it scaffolds the story. It might help you make sense of all the chaos."

The newsroom where she works, the newsroom that she loves, has become inaccessible to someone like her: three kids underfoot and a husband circling the globe. Her hero had insisted on the move to suburbia, two months before. He said it would give the girls more legroom and green space, give himself two more shortcuts to the airport—better odds of spending "quality" time with the family when he was in town since the quantity was not in danger of shrinking. Her hero insisted even though the three now go to two different schools—the Eldest and the Youngest didn't want to switch to the new school and tanked their entrance exams so well that the admissions officer sent a handwritten note recommending they be held back a year to "catch up." The Middle wasn't so cunning, and for the past two months they've been rising before the moon dips back into the horizon, just to beat traffic on the interstate; and in the afternoons, Mother sits in the longest car line recorded in North America.

In her hero's absence: too many channels on the radio and television but nothing really worth watching or listening to, too many news stories about wars and famine and desolation, too many flora and fauna reaching extinction, too many thoughts, too many good intentions, too many regrets, too many words left to write. Not enough hours. There's all that.

Then there's the black hole in her stomach expanding every time she hears or reads about the wars and famine and the extinctions, the road rages, the police state emerging, routine traffic stops that turn into massacre, the Bible Belt expanding at the waistline of the data-obese nation, a cacophony of voices rebuking. The voices are inside her mind but sound suspiciously like her grammar teacher in the seventh grade, Mrs. Griffith, who failed her for correcting the teacher's aide's grammar; and then her ninth-grade science teacher, Mrs. Whitfield, who did not like her and made a point of telling her so every class period. "When are you going back to your own country? When?" She wonders what circle of Dante's hell the world will resemble when her daughters are grown.

She turns the page of the borrowed book and begins to read.

&

A dog's sharp bark reverberates. A dog that is hungry.

&

She wants to write, and does. She turns down the volume on the radio, so she can concentrate. All that flows from her pen is a memory, a moment that she can appreciate only now that she's miles and years from it:

> Quiet as the forest in the heat of the day. A long moment of respite from the toys and the games and the preparations and the activities and the cleanups. This house, this old house, cool in the summer and cooler in the winter, the babies all sleeping, their stomachs slightly distended from their midday meals, the bottles of milk they gravitate to the way sunflowers do every morning, as they stand tall and face the sun. She listens on their monitors and hears their gentle snores and puts a finger to her lips as her shepherd smiles; shepherd's teeth showing as she shakes herself awake and wanders through the doors shaped like Old West saloon doors, and sniffs her bowl, looking for something else to eat. Her hero home from another overseas journey, snoring in his bed, shades drawn. She follows her shepherd into the kitchen and pulls out a bowl of cut fruit

from the fridge, a bowl of leftover brown
rice and chicken curry out of the beeping
microwave. She shares with her shepherd,
laughing as she tosses a cube of cantaloupe
high into the air and Greta leaps perfectly
and swallows her prize whole.

&

The wind rubbernecks and she shivers on the driveway.

&

He is helping her into the white dress with eyelet flowers. The hospital room walls are white, too, as are the bars of fluorescent light overhead. "It doesn't matter." He zips her up.

She cries as she steps into the matching sandals, and bends down ever so slightly to pick up her purse from the foot of the raised bed. "It means everything."

He shakes his head. "No," he says, his blond hair uncombed, blond stubble on his cheeks. "It's just one thing."

Children are the most precious gifts a couple can give to each other, she can hear her grandmother's voice echoing in Bengali from long ago. Don't wait too long. "Our families," she says, counting to herself more than six and a half years since their grand wedding in India. "Everyone will be disappointed."

He shrugs. "We have Greta."

She laughs and her stomach hurts. "I don't think our parents had that in mind as a legacy."

He smiles. "We're happy, right?"

She shivers, she nods.

"Then we have everything." He holds open the door. "I'm not worried."

She swallows. "My hero."

&

An owl hoots a second question, then falls silent as the armed agents stomp on the grass and through the front door, their boots unsynchronized percussion.

&

The Youngest Daughter, who says she wants to live in the backyard under a pair of presently perished and pulped cedars, asks, "Can I go back to my room now?" It is a muggy July 4, and the mosquitoes are the size of monarch butterflies. Never mind that the Youngest throws the mother of all temper tantrums twice a day—a package deal complete with shouting and pelting objects, like her Queen of Hearts deck of cards, across the room, pegging the Eldest Daughter squarely between the eyes. Never mind that she wakes up the Middle Daughter from a much-needed nap and causes Mother's brain to explode in a migraine. Never mind that she takes a sticky note with important phone numbers out of her father's hands, balls it up, and pops it in her mouth for a quick snack. Never mind that her parents are ready to put each other up for adoption rather than listen to their child complain once more.

Never mind that five days after the move into the new house lightning strikes the two cedar trees in the backyard, jumps the electric fence that was especially installed to keep the dog from running away (once she is brought home from the kennel), and leaves a gaping wound in the garage—no power, no telephone, no TV, no Internet, no way to close the garage doors, no way to keep things cold in the fridge, no way to wash clothes, no alarm, no normalcy until a brigade of repairmen complete their tasks and everything sort of looks like it did before.

Except for the trees.

&

She cannot see, her eyes will not open. But her ears work overtime, and she listens: the sound of the policemen's bodies walking past her toward the smooth asphalt street. "Sir? Sir? Yes, you. What's your name? Kurt? Curtis? . . . Okay, Curtis, please set up your equipment right over there. Sir? On the sidewalk. That's public property."

&

The new neighborhood, a subdivision gated by iron and brick, is shaped like a Picasso body. Two dozen houses make up the cubist form. It's the esophagus, a cul-de-sac with a small man-made lake that is the scene of a strange fire one Tuesday night.

Three separate fire trucks come as well as two ambulances. Yet only a wisp of smoke and no official fire. No one at home and no indication that anybody actually lives there full-time—no clothes in the closets, no toys or books in the children's rooms, no crumbs or untidiness to indicate a day-to-day existence. Some wooden furniture, a few cups and dishes in the kitchen cupboards. But the inside looks like a Barbie time-share condominium by the beach, not a family home in the neighborhood. Of course, the neighbors turn out for this spectacle. No one says anything, no one answers her question, asked in a myriad of ways: What happened here? All avert their eyes as she turns her head from one side of the crowd to the other, to gaze upon them, to see them, to be seen. Yet no one sees, no one chooses to see.

&

The question can be stripped bare, a striped white line on the
highway separating those stuck in traffic from those who are
flying down the road: Has anything of significance changed
in the last forty-three years?

&

The family is at the new park on Sunday afternoon. All three girls are side by side on the swings and her man of the hour, who has made blueberry pancakes for breakfast and homemade extra-cheese pizza for lunch, is also a master swing pusher. He pushes all three girls while she holds up Olympic-style scores for each push on the back of her notebook paper. Every push is scored a 10. He is leaving for a two-week stint in Japan the following day.

"You're easy to please," he says, laughing.

"My hero," she says. "Every push you give is one less push I have to give."

A couple with a toddler boy walk by, put their child in the last baby swing on the end. The woman turns to her hero and says, "What pretty girls you have."

He winks at his wife. "Thank you."

Mother asks the other woman, "How old is your child?"

"This one is almost two, and we have an older boy over there," the other mother says, pointing with her pale hand, a diamond glistening on her ring finger, matching the studs in her ears.

A game of playground math. "How old is he?"

The other woman says a number then laughs, and corrects herself. "Well, he'll be that old next Tuesday when he has his birthday party."

"She's that age," Mother says, pointing to the Youngest.

"She's so petite," the woman says. She looks over all of them, again. "They're all so petite. I bet it's all tea parties and dolls and sugar at your house."

Her hero smiles. "We do have our share of trucks and blocks and robots," he says, continuing to push.

"You're so outnumbered. Are you going to try for a son now?"

"No," he answers. "I like being the only king of the house."

"You say that now, but don't you want to play football with your son one day? Don't you want to be able to watch him play?"

He smiles slowly, and the smile doesn't quite reach his eyes. "Thanks to Title Nine, I can watch my girls play the other futbol, I can cheer them on."

Mother feigns a yawn to mask her smile. Her hero is so unlike everyone else in her personal and professional orbit.

INCITING INCIDENTS

. . . in which the narrator attempts to decide which particular incident set her on the path of this particular life story, concrete driveway and all, without sprinkling regret and bitterness over everything upon which she stews, without uttering the word *no* . . .

&

Possibly the exact moment the mustached state policeman, in monogrammed Kevlar and matching navy pants, stands in her driveway and points his assault rifle at her head on a cloudless morning in May, right after she took the girls to school, before she has her shower, and while she is still wearing her brown "Hard Work Never Killed Anyone But Why Risk It?" T-shirt and gray sweatpants.

Possibly one minute later when she counts the number of police and the number of automatic guns on her front lawn: all weapons at the ready as if she would cower before them or be impressed at the demonstration of force or be more inclined to listen to their list of demands.

Possibly a moment not too much later when the firecrackers are unexpectedly displayed, and she finds herself on the ground, bleeding.

&

Perhaps it is in the space of the moment two years before the men in bulletproof vests show up, when the vet stares at her directly in the eye and says, "You have to put her down." Dr. Graham's tone is quiet the way her subdivision remains hushed during the school day when the neighborhood kids aren't around yelling at one another about who cheated whom in some sketchy game of chance.

The three of them in a room the size of a broom closet. Chilled by the AC like the morgue.

As if she could ever kill Greta.

As if she could ever have her killed.

"It's not that bad," she says. She is Greta's human mother. She and her hero rescued Greta a decade before.

The vet's face is pale and her eyes drop down to the tired Mother's thighs as the German shepherd inches closer, panting in the cold room, the cold tip of her nose touching the pant leg. "Just look at her," Dr. Graham says. "Really look."

She, the human mother, the rescuer, drops down to her knees and catalogs what Greta endures without sound— paws curling in from a degenerative disease, toenails bleeding, naps longer and longer, coat shedding in large clumps, meals imaginary.

Greta licks her lips and plants her mom a kiss.

&

Or, years earlier, the moonless night before she goes into labor for the first time, the air thick with mosquitoes. Hands, face, and feet swollen from gestational diabetes. She wears flip-flops everywhere, the police precincts, the courthouses she covers, and the newsroom where she works as a journalist. For months, all jewelry had been off her hands, ears, and neck to quell the tide of swelling, the tide that never ebbs. The dangerous pregnancy and its forty daily admonitions and precautions always looping in succession in her mind. Labor Day weekend, 1998. After work, she lives in black stretch pants and a maternity T-shirt that has a cartoon picture of Garfield on it because those are the only two comfortable things she owns.

It is close to midnight and neither her husband nor she can sleep. So humid that even the crickets in the Georgia thickets stop chirping to conserve personal energy. They decide to watch a movie, but notice there is no popcorn, her only ob-gyn-approved snack, left in the pantry. She volunteers to go to the 24-hour grocery a few miles away to lap up the hyper-air-conditioned air, while her husband, her hero, tries his luck at renting *Titanic*.

A beached whale trying to navigate the aisles with a shopping cart, she remembers to take advantage of her human hands. She enjoys the forced air-conditioning, relishes the empty aisles and stocked shelves. She picks out her popcorn, and for her husband she chooses a variety of tasty garbage including a pint of ice cream that is called, appropriately enough, Coma by Chocolate.

One checkout lane open. Manned by a man named Manny who, according to his name tag, is the night manager. She looks like she is carrying some sort of obscene food baby ex utero, chips and popcorn for the torso and legs, chocolate chip cookies for the pair of arms joined together, and ice cream for the head.

He gawks. "Ma'am, do you know about prenatal care? There are some vitamins on Aisle Twelve, next to the baby wipes."

She turns around but finds herself alone. "Excuse me?"

He cocks his head. "Hables español?"

"What?" She gulps. "Yes, but . . . no."

"Ma'am, you need to put back the chips and the ice cream, and drink some milk."

She attempts to clamp shut her jaw but fails. "It's for my husband."

"Are you kidding me?" He pounds his fist on the price scanner. "What kind of man allows his pregnant wife to go to the store in the middle of the night?"

"I didn't want to go to the video store." She swipes the credit card. "It smells in there."

He grunts. "Are you sure you're married?"

A small hiccup of laughter escapes. "Why?"

"Where's your ring?" His stare almost a glare. "People will talk."

"At home."

"Where's your house?" His finger wags near her face.

"Three miles that way," she says, pushing away his hand.

"Do you have a doctor?"

"Actually, I have two." She signs the promissory note and waits. "And I have a medical condition that prevents me from eating anything after dinner, except for this popcorn I've bought."

"Bless your heart, ma'am," he says. "I'm just concerned for you."

Huh. "That's excruciatingly touching."

"Excuse me?"

"Can I have my receipt now? Please?" Nothing has changed. The dolls are still judged. She is thirty-one years, ten months, and six days old.

&

Perhaps it is the last day she is a resident of Manhattan. Two glorious years in New York, graduate school, she and Emily and Lydia practically inseparable. She leaves the last two boxes of books—poetry, biography, some novels, a coffee-table book on the history of art—on the doorstep of another classmate, Sarah, who is lucky to live near the *Seinfeld* diner year-round. Emily waits at the nearby coffeehouse, for the final goodbye, to cement the promise that they'd always be sisters, that they'd stay in touch. Her flight to California is later that night. Lydia is leaving the following day, for Chicago; and she is heading to Georgia, with the official designation as trailing spouse. The Real Thing walks into the shop, and finds Emily alone at the table set for three. "Where's Ly?"

Emily grimaces. "She couldn't stay."

"What? She's not going to say goodbye?"

"Not everyone is good at goodbye," Emily says. "Not everyone is as practiced as you."

&

Or, years later, after she moves them from the city to homogeneous suburbia, cookie-cutter identical for everyone but her. No one answers their doors when mother and daughters march up and down the cul-de-sac and ring the doorbells, homemade brownies in hand. Not only do the new neighbors not come over to see if they are all right after the lightning strikes the new house, none of them bother to say welcome. No chicken casseroles forthcoming, no chocolate chip or oatmeal cookies, no smiles. They, the family, wait patiently, every day, like maiden aunts at a charity dance, waiting to be asked to waltz.

No one calls.

&

Or the inciting incident might have begun when the Real Thing was really young. No one else in that part of North Carolina wants a brown-skinned doll with big brown eyes and black curls soft as silk ribbons. "She looked just like you. You were the same size," her own mother says. "I had to get her."

It is 9 p.m., Tuesday night. Her father behind the wheel of a used Chevy Nova, metallic green. Her mother riding shotgun. No car seats back then. So the Real Thing is sitting in her mother's lap and the baby doll is sitting in the Real Thing's lap. Dawn-pink dress, dusk-blue sash.

Inverted nesting dolls.

"Green lights all the way home," her mother likes to say. Her parents congratulating each other on their good fortune, a quick trip home. Except that the traffic light at the intersection of Franklin Street and Estes Drive turns yellow and then bright red before her father can react. He presses the brake hard, hard, hard. All the dolls fly. The Real Thing and her doll springboard from laps to crack the windshield.

"I was wearing white," her mother says. "By the time we got to the hospital, it was red-and-pink batik."

The Real Thing has ten stitches and a concussion, and the doll loses her head.

&

Maybe, just maybe, it all starts one morning in the fall semester, 1986, when she meets her man of the hour and coins
her nickname for him. The starting line for the hard looks
and comments that will follow them for the next twenty-four
years, strangers unhappy when they hold hands or kiss in
public. That Friday, the leaves burnishing gold and crimson
and copper among the evergreens, the air brisk even in the
afternoon. It is her turn to feed the meter, not just for her
clunker, but for her roommate, Donna, as well. The meter
maids on campus have been cracking down and the Real
Thing knows she cannot afford yet another parking ticket.
She is in danger of losing her car, her parents had warned her
it would be confiscated if one more parking offense reached
their mailbox, and without her car, well, she will lose her
part-time job as a newbie reporter in the local bureau of the
second-largest newspaper in the state of North Carolina.

Her English professor, Dr. Shelley, had let them out late,
nine and a half minutes late. An entire semester devoted to
the verses of John Donne, one ecstatic poem after the other,
a graduation requirement. The professor's voice more irritat-
ing than her fuchsia-painted nails that accidentally scratch
the chalkboard as she writes out her lecture during class.
In her haste to reach the cars before the meter maids do,
the Real Thing trips over a brick paver by the planetarium
entrance and the quarters fly from her fingers into the laby-

rinth of rosebushes. She spies one, and scratches her left arm on the thorns as she retrieves it.

The meter maid is six, maybe seven, cars away from her hatchback but only a few cars from her roommate's. Her trot turns into a jog, backpack slung over one shoulder, toward her roommate's white Chevy Cavalier. She stops at the car, and notices that beside it is its twin. The meter maid is two cars away. She dashes to the back of the car, but the license plates are virtually the same, and each car is sporting identical university magnets and business school logos.

The meter maid is close enough that the Real Thing could reach out and touch her cap. She reaches the meter, and puts in the quarter, and buys another hour.

"Thank you for rescuing my cadaver," a voice says by her ear.

"What?" She looks up to see the chiseled jaw, the brightest blue eyes, a bemused grin. "Wait, did I pay for your car?"

"Yes," he says, and introduces himself, tells her he's named the car a cadaver because it often fails to start in cold weather. "Are you okay? I saw you fall back there."

The Real Thing feels a cinnamon-red blush flooding her face. "I'm trying to beat the meter maid, for my roommate."

"Allow me," he says, and fishes for something in his pocket but comes up empty. The grin fades as he looks on the ground and on the curb. "Damn it."

"What's wrong?" she asks, aware of the meter maid inching closer.

"I thought I had an extra coin or two," he says, then

looks closely at a spot just above her shoulder. He tucks a strand of hair behind her ear and produces a quarter, tucks another strand, and produces three. "I knew they were here somewhere."

He feeds one of the quarters into Donna's Chevy.

The Real Thing laughs. "You're the man of the hour!" She snatches the remaining coins from his hand and runs to her car, feeds her own meter as well as the meters of the cars on either side of her. She looks back to see her new friend speaking to the meter maid, a small white package in his hand, and then the maid hopping back into her vehicle and moving toward the exit. She walks back to him. "What did you say to her?"

He shrugs and shows her his roll of quarters. "I promised her I'd feed everyone's meter."

She wonders why he has this money, and remembers the arcade just down the block. "And she believed you?"

His smile holds the glow of a campfire in the deep woods.

She pictures herself as a moth.

"She's coming back in fifteen minutes, to check." He breaks the roll in half. "You'll keep me honest, right?"

She takes her half of the stack.

&

Perhaps it's when an older boy, Michael, follows Middle Daughter around during first-grade recess on the school playground, pushes her down in the hallway near the library, bumps her elbow in the cafeteria, calls her names that allude to the darker side of the color spectrum, calls her a coconut, white on the inside, for even wanting to attend this fancy Southern school. Michael gets on the cross-campus bus that transports the children to and from the school gymnasium and natatorium three days each week and sits behind her and taunts.

Middle Daughter announces her decision to forgo education for a life of flight. "I'll just go to the moon sooner than I thought," she says, breaking open a chocolate cookie and crumbling the sweet white frosting between her fingers. On TV, news anchors are showing NASA's photographs of the Phoenix soft landing on Mars.

"You have to finish high school, college, graduate school, a stint in the Air Force, and then NASA training," Mother says. She takes a sip of the black coffee and puts down the cup.

Middle Daughter's lower lip juts out, the cookie crumbles on the tabletop. "I just can't go to school anymore, not while HE is there."

Mother's heart crumbles too. "Can I tell Daddy now? Please?"

She shakes her head, unable to speak.

&

Perhaps it is the day of the Eldest's first bharatanatyam dance recital. Her hero is trying to fly back in time from Germany, but there is a severe snowstorm blanketing Western Europe and many flights have been delayed or canceled. The other daughters are quite small, and wearing matching red outfits in contrast to their big sister, who is wearing a blue sari, pleated and pinned just so. Everyone else is there, her in-laws, her parents, even the Baby Sister. So many hands offering to hold the babies, or fix the Eldest's makeup or hair. Mother uses her best honeyed voice, urging them to go sit on their grandparents' laps, play with their aunt. But the girls won't budge off Mother's lap, three girls refusing to concede, ignoring all the other adults, pulling each other's hair, crying loudly when they hear their father's voice on the speakerphone apologizing for the delay.

In the end, the little sisters are put to bed early and miss the recital, and the grandparents stay home to care for them, two grandparents for each little girl.

The Baby Sister and the Real Thing sit side by side in the first row, the Real Thing photographing every movement, the grace and ease with which the Eldest glides across the center of the stage.

&

Or when Editor Dennis sits her down for a talk, about a year after Greta dies. His homemade sweater vest stretches tightly across his nachos-and–Burger King stomach, which hangs like a precipice over his beige trousers. His hair is combed over but doesn't hide his soft pink scalp.

"It's nothing personal," the boss says.

His glasses are dark brown like what's left of his hair, and the lenses are thick like the glass bottom of a soda bottle. "You've always been able to adjust."

She is being demoted. As if that's even possible, since she is already part-time and working every miserable shift that no one else wants. She tries to remain stone-faced, looks past him toward the corridor, and sees that her game is up. Everyone is coming and going, the restrooms are Grand Central Station, so many faces and bodies that should be hurrying, hurrying, but no one is actually moving. Everybody is in the corridor, looking at her. Waiting. The watcher is being watched.

She coughs into her clenched fist. "What does this mean?"

Dennis shrugs. "You'll be more 'on call' with the news desk. I'm having to loan you out, they're shorthanded the next couple of months."

She calmly points out that she has children. Their smiles are frozen on her bulletin board. Her schedule is set in concrete. They cannot be left waiting in front of their schools. She is nothing if not religiously punctual. She has always beat the deadline.

The boss jiggles his right leg, his particular sign that he is nervous and needs to go outside for a smoke. The sweater vest is wiggling in time. "You don't have to work here, you know."

She forces her shoulders back. "I'm the best reporter you have for this job."

He smiles. "Yes," he concedes. He pulls out a cigarette and a bright blue lighter. He lights the cigarette, it smells like cloves. Not his usual brand. She glances past him again, toward the corridor, and sees that the crowd has largely dispersed. Yet the assistant copy editor for the night staff is staring intently. Her golden hair is pulled back into a French braid. Mother stumbles through a corridor of memory, and tries to catch the copy editor's name.

Lyn. No, not quite. Lynette. Lynette, who couldn't hold her liquor at the Christmas party two years before, who threw up in the women's bathroom shortly before midnight, but kept drinking, kept dancing by herself to the live band, long after the couples had left.

She waves at Lynette, and says to her boss, "I think your friend is waiting for you."

His face turns as pink as his scalp. "They can't fire me for smoking."

"But they can fire you for smoking inside."

He laughs, then coughs. He stands up and waves toward

the City Desk. The sweater vest is bunched up over his stomach, like a toddler's. "You're wanted over there."

She waits until he and Lynette get on the elevator. She looks into the eyes of her children, frozen on the bulletin board, and touches their sweet, smiling faces. She pushes her chair back into the desk, begins walking, past the evacuation routes posted on the wall, in case the building is on fire. The only time she's ever seen anyone study them was on 9/11, when the national reporters crowded around the placards and pointed with their chewed-up ballpoints. "Maybe they got out, maybe they got out. Look at these directions, they're very detailed."

None of their friends got out that day. She remembers that it was her last day in the newsroom before the second maternity leave, her boss at the time unhappy he had to give her eight weeks off. "I don't know if I can hold the job," he'd said. "There are six people here who want it." But the job was waiting for her when she returned. She'd hung on.

&

Perhaps when the women in the neighborhood refuse to look at her. She remembers driving past them. She remembers them averting their heads. Before she reached her driveway she ping-pongs between the idea that she is driving to her death, and that she is a widow—that her hero had already driven to his demise. Then a short time later, the owl that has been hanging out in the backyard emitting its third hoot-hoot at the sound of the shot. She cannot open her eyes but the heat of the sun is crawling down her body, and the pain in her stomach persists. She hears the neighborhood women's familiar-unfamiliar voices and pictures them watching the spectacle like a reality-TV show.

She jumps to the moment years before when she was sitting down to watch an interview on the employee lounge TV, in her lap the sandwich her hero had packed that morn-ing, Iberian ham with sharp white Vermont cheddar. She unwraps the wax paper and lifts the sandwich to take a bite, when the cell phone rings. Her hero. She answers and he is in a rush to speak, does not bother with a greeting: "Please tell me you haven't had lunch yet."

She answers that she is about to take her first bite, and she can hear the relief in his laughter.

"Don't," he pleads. "I forgot to take the paper off the cheese."

Apparently thin nearly translucent squares of white paper were inserted in between the white cheddar slices, for convenience in separation of one part from the whole.

"My hero," she says, "my hero sandwich." She giggles, removes the top slice of bread, takes the white paper off the cheese and most of the mayo with it.

"You dodged a bullet," he says. "You could have choked."

She starts to laugh but stops. "Is that what happened to you?"

&

In this new neighborhood the wives take baths (not showers), put on pumps, and apply mascara just to retrieve the morning newspapers from the edge of the driveway or check the mail before their children come home from school. Their husbands take notice of other things, and leave curt messages duct-taped to the front door of Mother's house. Her man of the hour is usually not home, he is usually out of town for work. But her man of the hour happens to be at home when the latest note about their failings as residents of the subdivision, on cut yellow Post-it, is posted.

"We have to be nice," he says, softly, as he sits down next to her on the couch. "We agreed to follow their rules when we moved here."

Greta is by the fireplace, and she opens her eyes. She wags her tail weakly but does not sit up.

"A lightning strike. We couldn't close the doors to the garage." Mother pokes holes in the yellow Post-it with a ballpoint pen. "Everything was broken."

Her hero turns on the TV and finds a college basketball game. "They don't care."

She looks at the box, the score is tied. "But we couldn't park in the driveway. The repairmen were parked there." The pen breaks the skin of the paper and goes through.

He starts to channel surf. "They don't care."

She puts her hand out and they trade, note and pen for

remote. "They didn't even check on us when we were hit! We could have had a fire. We could have died."

He crumples the paper into a ball and puts the cap back on the pen, and then juggles them high into the air. Greta takes notice and her head follows the paper ball like an avid tennis fan at Wimbledon.

Mother finds *The Wizard of Oz*, it is the moment that Dorothy falls asleep in the field of poppies. Greta rises and wobbles to Mother's side of the couch, sits back down again. They all watch in silence until a mouthwash commercial interrupts the film just as Dorothy and her companions enter the Emerald City.

Her hero sighs. Maybe in resignation. "If we fight this, we'll end up in court. They'll have the law, and then we'll have to apologize and we'll have to pay a fine."

They trade again. She tucks the pen behind her ear, and makes a perfect shot with the Post-it into the wastepaper basket on the other side of the couch. Greta follows the shot and goes to investigate the trash can. Mother says, "I just think we should . . ."

Her hero changes the channel back to the basketball game. Overtime. "Be nice," he says. "By the way, I have to go out of town again."

&

Mattel claims that more than one billion Barbie dolls have sold in one hundred and fifty countries—that a Barbie is sold every three seconds. In the time it takes her to close the pages of the Barbie encyclopedia and place it on the cart for reshelving, another thirty Barbie dolls are sold.

She races through time, to her undergraduate days, to the auditorium with the red velvet curtains, to the naturalist who came to the university and spoke of butterflies and moths. He estimated there were 17,000 butterfly species in the world at that time, and that more than 300,000 butterflies came through the three Cs—caterpillar, cocoon, and chrysalis—every year. He estimated that they lived two to seventeen days, that their time on earth was spent living, that butterflies don't sleep. He said the monarchs were the exception, that they lived about six months—that they lived long enough to make the journey home to the place where they would die.

&

The Bengali grandmothers' midnight folktales, kitchen superstitions, follow her still, like birds. The cautions and precautions as she sat, feet dangling from her chair at their kitchen tables eating sandesh sweetened by khejuur guur, to now, her legs twisted awkwardly under her, blood in her mouth. How, when the butterflies in the botanical gardens in Calcutta swarmed the Real Thing but not the Baby Sister, her great-aunt predicted that the Baby Sister would not marry.

How their grandfather, jailed for resisting the British Raj, lived through famine and Partition, always said: Never leave rice on your plate, for it will bring you hunger. The look on her hero's face as she repeated Dadu's words and ate every bite the girls left on their plates at the Thai restaurant, thirty years later. "Why are you doing this? You said you were full," her hero says, signaling the waiter for the check. "You don't have to eat this."

And the one admonition she'd heard from all of the elders, on both sides of the family, even her parents: Never buy a loved one a pair of shoes, for you'll invite their departure. Her hero leaving his wallet at home one Saturday early in their marriage, before Saturday outings with her hero became rare, and her refusal to buy him high-tops at the mall near downtown Honolulu.

"It's just an old wives' tale," he says. "You don't have to believe it."

But the Real Thing counters with the story of the Baby Sister convincing their parents to buy her soccer cleats, and then two years later, after high school, leaving the family, joining the church. The Real Thing is always writing down connections, however ephemeral, between the myths of her childhood India trips and her stark American life.

Her hero fusses, and finally she relents and buys him not one, but two pairs of shoes. The receipt is chalk-blue colored and the ink on the slip is thin and red like a trickle of blood.

And now she can't help but believe it, how she's driven her hero away with that purchase, now that she's been essentially alone for years, how the prajapati and the juta conspired to separate her from her sister.

&

More likely, it began on the playground when Mary-Margaret Anne Moriarty expounded on her theory of love. Recess, at St. Luke's co-ed. Last full week of April 1978. A day when the azaleas are already in bloom, when sixth grade still means elementary school, and the term "middle school" hasn't yet replaced "junior high." While other schoolkids embrace the Bee Gees and John Travolta, the Real Thing and her classmates argue with nuns about attending mandatory morning mass, even as non-Catholics. On the playground Sister Joan drones on about school uniforms, which look suspiciously like habits except they are an ugly green plaid, and how their souls would be in mortal danger if "boys" could see the girls' knees or calves or shins or even ankles. She wants to know what mortal danger really means but doesn't understand the correlation between that and her bony kneecaps—scarred by the rough tumble off her bike in the woods near the creepy cemetery managed by the Bible thumpers who want to save her soul but know better than to ring the doorbell and argue with her mother once more. The school bell rings, calling them back to their classrooms.

Mary-Margaret Anne, as she likes to be called, stands two feet away from her. Dirty blond with tiny pixie freckles sprinkled across the bridge of her bulbous nose. Her father is a businessman who is never in town except on Friday afternoons, when he picks up Mary-Margaret Anne from school

In a white Mustang convertible. Her mother roams in a station wagon with three boys still in diapers, rolling down the window at the curb, begging Mary-Margaret Anne to get in. And Mary-Margaret Anne never hurries her pace, and finishes speaking to Ellen and Paige and Jeanette before strolling to the car and flinging her hot-pink bag into the trunk. The Moriarty parents never offer the Real Thing a ride, but drive by as she trudges past the firehouse and an abandoned wooden structure with a caved-in porch that even animals stay away from, to the city bus stop a half mile away. Monday through Friday. Rain, shine, sleet, snow, like the postman. The boy Mary-Margaret Anne is "going" with, Eric Moynihan, has ignored his girlfriend that morning but utters "excuse me" as he whizzes by on his way back to his seat, his blurry form jostling the Real Thing's left arm. Mary-Margaret Anne's eyes flash green in the sunlight. "What did he say?"

"Nothing," she replies, wishing she knew kung fu just then.

Mary-Margaret Anne pirouettes on her left foot, and she looks poised to do a jeté. She has the body to be a ballerina, and unlike her own mother, the Real Thing bets Mary-Margaret Anne's has no problems parting with the money, if only to get her daughter out of the house for a short time. "You know what I heard? I heard you and Henry have been kissing in the library during reading hour."

Sister Joan's head turns on her broad neck, like an owl. She stands equidistant from Mary-Margaret Anne and the

Real Thing and their shadows all lie flat on the blacktop. Sister Joan's stare through her thick spectacles is thoughtful.

Henry and his parents had moved to town from Michigan over Christmas.

He is the first Black boy at school. Well, his mother is Black but his father is white. And from where she sits, Henry is just another student. Hair neatly combed, pressed collared shirts, impeccably shiny shoes. Shiny copper pennies glistening from his penny loafers.

He never raises his hand.

He doesn't open his mouth.

She sits next to him, in the back of the room, watches him doodle battleships and helicopters on notebook paper during class, watches him crumple up the imperfect drawings and shoot hoops into the trash can, watches the nuns hand back perfect scores on his test papers. "I don't think so," she says, picturing Mary-Margaret Anne's head in a guillotine, like the one she read about in history after an unflattering description of Marie-Antoinette. "He's never even said hello."

Mary-Margaret Anne's grin is all knowing, the way her lips spread thinly over her even teeth. It is the same smile that she produces when she talks loudly to Ellen and Paige and Jeanette about how she and Eric are one day going to "do it" when her mother isn't at home; and that after she "did it" with Eric, he would have to marry her. She can only imagine what "it" is, and judging from the bewildered look in Paige's hazel eyes, their classmate doesn't know either.

"It's okay, you don't have to tell me," Mary-Margaret Anne says. "But it's nice that you two are going together."

Sister Joan raises her eyebrows, and through the magnification of her glasses they look like perfectly synchronized caterpillars doing aerobics.

She shakes her head. "We're not going together."

Mary-Margaret Anne shrugs. "It makes sense."

It does not. "Why?" she asks, pinching her fingers together so she won't shout at Mary-Margaret Anne in front of Sister Joan and spend another afternoon in Sister Grace's musty headmistress office hearing about her lack of gratitude for being "taken" off the streets—although she doesn't quite understand what streets she is being spared from, since she still has to walk a half mile every weekday to and from the city bus stop to school.

"He's Black," says Mary-Margaret Anne, a coo at the back of her throat.

No, actually the color of his skin is coffee with cream. Since he never smiles, it is coffee sans sucre. "I'm not Black."

"Sure you are," she says. "You're not white."

The Real Thing feels hot in her face but knows she can never cry in front of Mary-Margaret Anne, or she will never be able to come back to school again.

Sister Joan's head turns back to a forward position, her step takes on a definite marching intonation. She simply enters the building and disappears.

"Nobody," Mary-Margaret Anne says, enunciating the

first syllable at twice the length it normally requires, "like Eric will ever ask you to go with him."

The Real Thing pinches her palm as hard as she can and the ocean of tears at the eyelid shores recede. "Why not?"

"Because," Mary-Margaret Anne says, suddenly touching her skin, creating a crater of shock, "this doesn't rub off."

ACT I:

THE CURTAINS ARE DRAWN, BRIEFLY

. . . in which she resolves not to let it bother her, the loneliness, the responsibility, the nagging inner critic who uses a bullhorn to broadcast into her inner ear she cannot manage everything, that she cannot manage anything, that it is all her own doing, her undoing that is. Her hands begin to tremble . . .

&

Can she stop wishing for change? Can she stop hoping?

&

Barbie was originally conceived as a working girl, career-minded, trailblazing. For example, Miss Astronaut Barbie came alive in 1965, and Doctor Barbie was born in 1987, and NASCAR Barbie drove onto the scene eleven years later, in 1998. Not that she got to play with any of those dolls. But still.

&

She is three, on the cusp of four. Her birthday party is around the corner, where the neighbor's daughter from across the street, the one who lived in a white split-level that looked a lot like the *Brady Bunch* house, will pull her hair. The neighbor's daughter will also complain about the strawberry cake and the too-sweet pink frosting and her mother's face will crumple in the bathroom once the guests leave. But in this moment, she is three again, almost four. The TV is on in the next room, a large outdoor concert, and a guitarist plays what she will come to know as "The Star-Spangled Banner." She and her mother are in the kitchen, she is dancing on the linoleum that is printed to resemble red bricks, and her mother is cooking dinner on the front two burners. She likes the carousel feeling of twirling on the linoleum, it is so much faster in the kitchen than on the thick-carpeted floors of her bedroom or the TV room. Her mother cautions her not to get too close to the stove, the front two coils are angry and almost as red as the linoleum. Once, twice, three times. And she smiles and keeps dancing. The telephone rings. She reaches the stove, and her mother quickly turns off the burners. Her mother spins around and grabs her by the shoulders. "Stay right there," she says, her dark eyes shining fear. "I have to get that." Her mother goes toward the sink, the electric coils hissing slightly as they return to their inactive onyx state. They are so pretty, so shiny as she leans close. The Real Thing takes her pointer finger and gently dots the outermost coil, already black: she jumps back as the heat registers on her fingertip.

&

"I will never forget how she behaved," her mother says, bitterness condensing her voice like a thick soup. "She" is the Baby Sister, now all grown up and far from home. Their mother scrubs the pan harder, the Brillo pad a scratchy percussion on the bottom of the burned pan. The kitchen smells of cumin seeds that have blackened and look like cracked peppercorn, spicy yet inedible. "Hurtful," she says, "not even considering how we might have felt then, how we had a right to be grieved hearing the news."

The once-upon-a-time Baby Sister must have told their mother to stop whining and acting like a child. Another grievance. It could be a grievance from earlier in the week when a six-year-old beauty queen was found murdered in her family home in Colorado, it could be a grievance from when *Saturday Night Fever* was playing at the movie theater down the street decades ago. Time was fluid in the long list of past grievances.

"No two snowflakes are ever alike," the remaining, acknowledged daughter says, staring out the bay window, the snow falling calm and white over the barren trees, the barren ground. An icy blanket. Winter remains the Baby Sister's favorite season.

Their mother twists the tap handle as if she were driving a car and making a sudden left turn. The water gushes out and runs like the wind chimes in the neighbor's back patio. She jams shut the lever with her elbow and puts the newly scrubbed pan in the dish rack. "I have tomato soup and sourdough bread for lunch."

A sigh.

Everyone in the family knows the allergies and intolerances have reared their gorgon heads, and neither tomatoes nor whole wheat are part of the prescribed foods. "I can't eat that," the Real Thing says.

Their mother pivots from one leg to another. "Well, I can't make a second lunch." Her tone is as flat as the granite surface of the counter. She stirs the pot, resting atop a black coil. "You know that. Why do you expect me to make you a second lunch?"

Another sigh. The Real Thing eyes the car keys on the kitchen table next to her wallet. She walks over, scoops up everything as if she were scooping forbidden ice cream onto a forbidden waffle cone, and saunters toward the front door. "I won't be long," she says.

"You're not going to eat with me?"

"I can't," she says. "I forgot, I have a lunch date." With the Baby Sister, on a pay phone at the mall.

"In this weather?" Their mother rushes toward the window. "Cancel it! Just make do with what we have at home."

But the once-upon-a-time Real Thing is already out the door. She is home in North Carolina visiting, taking time off from her newspaper job in Hawaii to address their mother's sudden new ailment, but spending every moment as far from the cacophony as she can.

&

The dispatcher squawks, "Hollis, come again. I didn't hear you."

&

The answer shall always remain the same. The short answer is no. It is followed by a longer answer: No way. It is followed further by a litany: No how. No chance. Not on your life. Never.

&

There is the extra-long answer: Not as long as she has breath left in her poor, tired, broken-down, enraged, disgraced, exhausted body.

&

There. There's the first emergency exit, and there's the metal-barred door that leads to the platform and then to the women's bathroom. The line is snaking purposefully toward the open throat of the tunnel that leads to the ride, available exclusively inside the California theme park. Appropriately named Hell on Earth. Antigravity, multiple 360-degree turns. Guaranteed you'll wish you weren't born. How could the little girls want to do this? How could she have agreed? Her hero grins for the first time since Greta died, and her stomach drops down the three stories to street level, where the watching spectators already look small, doll-like. She and her family walk past the last emergency exit. "I'm going to throw up," she hears herself whispering.

The Eldest Daughter laughs. "You'll live, Mom."

&

The agent's eyes are the color of a bachelor's button, blue, but remote like the stars that make up Orion. He shows her the warrant. "I have the right to do this," he says, reiterating his desire to search her and her car. His desire. Her body. She looks past him for a second. Her front door is busted and armed agents are already inside her house.

She remembers her city editor Clay at the newspaper on O'ahu two jobs before, admonishing her when she had complained about a source's rudeness, the way the source had entered the Honolulu newsroom uninvited and wagged an accusing finger in her face. Shut the hell up, Clay's voice echoes. Do what you have to do to stay alive. Clay, whose actual voice she has not heard in years, Clay who is sick with a tropical ailment and sometimes cannot remember his own name. "No," she hears herself spewing, as if she were spitting out a mouthful of sand.

The female agent in charge points her finger. "We are the state police. We can do whatever we want."

"It's 2010," she hears herself arguing. "You can't."

The agent with the warrant backs her up to the car door, and his hands run down the length of her T-shirt and sweatpants, palms open, slowly as if there will be a pop quiz later on every square inch that he touches. "This is for my safety," he says, leaning close to her ear as if to whisper something tender. "What are you hiding?"

The female agent in charge looks down at her clipboard, pretending to study.

"It's 2010," Mother repeats. "You won't get away with this."

From the periphery of her eye she makes out the women, white on white and peroxide blond glistening in the Monday sun, aviators reflecting as they stand guard over the clipped grass and pressure-washed concrete, chess pieces waiting for the next move.

&

She spies Henry on the bus, sitting in between two young women, who look like college students. Sitting on bench seats in the back of the bus, the windows tinted blue, a placard advertising the university's collegiate apparel store in black and white above him. She does not recognize anyone on the crammed city bus except Henry, almost everyone else is reading the university newspaper on their laps, the front page showing a photograph of the now-nonexistent space shuttle *Challenger* shortly before takeoff. He sits squarely between the two brunettes, their white skin paling under their black jackets. The Real Thing, now all grown up, tries to say hello, she offers a smile as she sits across from him. He looks thin, all angles between his asymmetrical haircut and hollowed cheekbones, his skin especially ashy. He does not acknowledge her, his eyes are buttons on a worn peacoat.

She says, "Henry," softly, almost to herself.

He turns his head almost perpendicular to his body and he stares out the window. Someone pulls the cord, alerting the driver to take the next bus stop, near the corner of Franklin Street and Columbia, across from the church for which the town is named. She cannot stop staring, but finds her eyes starting to sting with rejection, and it is hard to keep her eyes open.

When the bus stops, the driver opens the doors. Henry takes the hand of the brunette on his left and exits.

Real Thing gulps the air and it is laced with bus exhaust.

She pulls the cord for the next stop, and stumbles as she gets off the bus.

She has to sit down at the curb, put her head between her knees.

&

Just maybe she changes right before her tenth birthday when she is forced to watch *The Pit and the Pendulum*. Teachers and staff herd all of the students in the third-, fourth-, and fifth-grade classes into the auditorium, turn on the projector, and then turn off the lights. The Baby Sister sits right behind her and buries her head between her didi's shoulder blades, and whimpers. They are spellbound, the way mice are hypnotized at the sight of a snake wriggling toward them. Vincent Price. Two hours. She doesn't recall much about the movie except for the dungeon. Oh yeah, she remembers the woman who is trapped inside the iron maiden. Her husband, played by Vincent Price, thinks her dead and buries her only to learn he'd killed her when he puts her in the family crypt. But mostly, the recollections center on sleeping with the lights on every night for a month. How unhappy their mother is with this new arrangement.

&

Just maybe she changes when the Baby Sister grows up and leaves the house for good. Just around the time the Mall of America opens in Minnesota and her once-upon-a-time shopaholic sister has renounced all the things found in malls. Her sister has renounced college, too. Her sister. Now a sister of God. Muslin habit. Periodic vows of silence.

&

In 1965, Slumber Party Barbie came with a weight scale permanently set at 110 pounds. On the "play scale," that would make Barbie a five-foot-nine woman who was 35 pounds underweight.

&

Just maybe she changes the first time (or the second or the third . . .) because she can't save even one of them. Eighteen months since the move, her hero out of town again. Since last Thursday, the Youngest Daughter walks around with a full plastic sandwich bag held to the side of her head. At first, there is ice in it, from when the Youngest bungee jumps off the top of the couch and Mother misses rescuing her by half a second. Now, when the Youngest discovers an empty plastic baggie, she fills it with crayons, animal crackers, squishy hair bands, cotton balls. She strolls from room to room, up and down the staircase, and in and out the front door, holding an extremely used plastic bag to her temple. Once in a while, she takes the baggie off of her head to inspect it and give it a small kiss, and then forces it to resume its position.

After the Youngest goes to bed, her mother cleans up the toys and occasionally finds a baggie. When her hero calls from his layover in Honolulu, Mother cradles the phone in one ear and puts the plastic bag, this one filled with broken animal crackers, to her temple.

These are examples of what it means to experience ghost pain.

&

The agents' voices dissolve into one another, forming an indistinct murmur. It is the sound the wind makes when it is dying down.

&

Just maybe she changes the day she is sent to the Happy Trails Trailer Homes & Community to interview a mother who survived the death of her children, and to gather materials for the children's obituary. An electrical fire that left a single mother burned on her elbows and stomach and knees for crawling to safety on a smoldering carpet, the toddler and infant in question dying from smoke inhalation. The grandmother opens the door to the neighbors' trailer and introduces her daughter, arms and legs wrapped in gauze, tongue wrapped in the aftereffects, no doubt, of sedatives and painkillers. "She wants to say something," the grandmother says, handing over a family portrait of the daughter and two granddaughters, in matching pink dresses and headbands; to give to the photographer who is taking pictures of the nearby scorched trailer. "She needs to." The grandmother's face is smooth and her skin is clear; the circles forming under her eyes will soon resemble matching bruises.

Real Thing looks at the young mother, and says as quietly as she can, "You don't have to."

The young woman cries, her straw-colored hair smells of a forest destroyed by fire. Her mascara runs. "I'm dead though my body is alive," she says. "I'll never get past this."

Real Thing looks at the woman and her mother. "You can't see it now, but one day you'll be able to," she says, trying to sound hopeful.

"I'm twenty-two," says the mother whose children will now sleep forever.

Real Thing looks down at her notebook and writes down *same age as me.*

&

A dog barks. It sounds like Greta. But Greta's been dead for almost two years.

&

Maybe she changes when she spends too much energy thinking about things she cannot change. Perhaps she spends entirely too much time replaying that one-sided conversation.
She knows the one, where the vet says Greta has a degenerative arthritic condition, that Greta's nerves are turning
into overcooked vermicelli, that it's just a matter of months
before all that will be left of her will be the ghost of her bark,
warnings her family will be unable to hear when outsiders
are drawing near.

&

What she wants to do is shake her head, like a bobble-head doll, and repeat, "No." But she can't move her neck, and cannot speak.

&

Her Greta, who doesn't live long enough to warn her when those agents begin banging their fists; when those agents swarm her house and yard like a battalion of wasps; when those agents raid her house and her body at gunpoint. Those agents whose questions about her hero don't stop.

&

Maybe she can still change the future.

"How come there are only dollhouses?" the Middle Daughter questions.

"Where are the doll schools?" the Eldest replies.

"Where are the doll temples and churches?"

"Where are their banks?" the Youngest asks. She always wins Monopoly, that one.

"What books do they read?"

"How come the only cars they drive are jeeps or convertibles?" the Eldest asks.

"How come all the boy dolls have clothes that mean they're either going to fight or going to work?" the Middle asks.

"Why are there a lot more clothes for girls?" the Eldest asks. "How come other people decide what clothes the girls get to wear? How come it says so on the box, right there?"

A pause. Toys strewn all over the family room floor, covering the carpet, creating a plastic minefield for those foolish enough to be walking around without their shoes. Raining. So no possibility of going outside to play. The unpacking of their lives into the new house remains under way. The water pelting the ground sounds like a generation of frustrated young girls beating the floor with their fists in protest of rules set long before they were born. Mother sits on the couch, surveying the landscape before her. The Youngest

Daughter, who has been watching in a trance, looks expectantly at her. Mother finally answers, "It's only a game."

The Youngest says, "But it's not fair."

"You can always change the game. You can always change their clothes."

"I know I can change them." The Eldest's tone is haughty, her chin and nose are high in the air. One day, after she conquers the world, that profile must go on the side of a coin. "That's not the point. Other people shouldn't tell us what to do with our own toys. Other people shouldn't make the toys without making all of the stuff that is supposed to go with it."

"That's part of the game," Mother says, her throat scratchy and worn as though beaten down by the fatigue of an unceasing cough. "Other people make the rules and you have to figure out how to break the rules without hurting anyone."

&

The object of the game, she decides suddenly, is not to lie in a pool of one's own blood.

&

In 1997, Barbie's tiny waist finally got remolded to fit with '90s fashions. For thirty-six years she was advised by Mattel to restrict her diet because the buttons and zippers and seams of her clothing were making her look "big."

&

Mother pulls out the license and registration. Again. Fourth time this week, first time on this stretch of road so close to the Department of Motor Vehicles, just after breakfast. One last errand and she's off to the car depot, the airport. California vacation on the horizon like the rising sun. The soft-boiled egg in her stomach scrambles and she tries not to gag when she sees the figure in her side-view, walking up to her. She does not say hello to the trooper, who bears an uncanny resemblance to David Crosby, the singer. In his hippie, drugged-out days when Neil Young was still part of the band, and Carter was still president.

"Do you know why we're here today?" The trooper's voice booms like a preacher on the mount, delivering brimstone before Sunday brunch. He snatches the documents from her and turns them over, as if she were an artist of the counterfeit variety.

She wants to answer but the scrambled egg has found shoes in her stomach, is lacing them up to make the hike back up her throat. She shakes her head.

"You could have killed yourself back there," he said, pointing with her documents to the start of the turn lane some fifty feet away.

Mother doesn't bother to look back or answer. She doesn't remember wanting to kill herself fifty feet ago. She stares straight ahead at the traffic light, changing from yellow to red. "I'm sorry," she says aloud, but regrets the apology, insincere and soaked in sarcasm, as it leaves her mouth. The egg has begun its Himalayan climb, and her stomach rumbles seismically in warning.

The trooper leans down so that his face is close enough for a slap. Or a kiss. She is doubly reflected in his aviator sunglasses. "Are you sassing me?"

She watches herself shake her head.

He straightens up. Maybe he smelled her breath, maybe he recognized that odor and knew to distance himself. "Don't move," he commands, before adjusting himself and ambling back to his vehicle.

She tries not to. She tries really hard, but then that egg. That goddamned soft-boiled egg, dash of pepper on top like an afterthought, she ate this morning.

It comes back to visit.

&

The sun tussles with a cloud and the glare dims for a moment. Goosebumps crop up all over. Her ears clog as if she were flying in the vacuum seal of an airplane. If only she could yawn and relieve the building pressure. But she cannot move, she is lying on her back and the concrete is cold.

She identifies this feeling as jet lag. The fog that comes when your mind recognizes that you've changed locations and circumstances but you're a body still living in the past.

&

Maybe she has misunderstood all along what the purpose of the telephone is. Her mother, the Grandmother, calls again. The same conversation, no matter the topic. The same topic, no matter the conversation. She is an Indian mother so the two focal points on this elliptical path are constant: food and weight. Mother and Grandmother have this conversation every week, ever since the children were born.

Grandmother asks, "Why don't you go to the gym? Why are the children so skinny? Why aren't you skinny like the children? Why are you cooking so much? Why aren't you cooking enough? Why are you wasting so much food? Did you eat the brownies I sent you? Why did you eat the brownies I sent you? You mean, you threw away the brownies I baked?"

She, Mother, stifles a yawn, and unpacks her artlike practice of sighing.

Sigh. Sigh. Sigh.

Sigh. Sigh.

Sigh.

Unfortunately for her, the day's last sigh is audible.

"I can't believe how disrespectful you have become," Grandmother says, voice as cold and remote as the very Himalayas she used to trek when she was younger and her daughters still children. "I can't believe you turned out this poorly."

&

The owl hoots again, a fourth question, a compound sentence, as if he has already forgotten the sound of the assault rifle being fired.

&

The questions are repetitive, a sound of gunfire rat-a-tat-tat.

How long have you lived here? rat-a-tat-tat. Your English is so good. When did you come over? rat-a-tat-tat. Who taught you? rat-a-tat-tat. Where? rat-a-tat-tat.

Her heartbeats answering, rat-a-tat-tat. "I'm American."

Yes, yes. Now, now. The answers come in pairs. Of course, of course. When did you take your citizenship test, again? rat-a-tat-tat, rat-a-tat-tat.

"At birth," rat-a-tat-tat, rat-a-tat-tat. The entirety of the near world now looking at her, looking through her. She clenches her fist briefly to stifle the eye roll, to stifle the sigh.

The questions change slightly, a spray of gunfire now deliberate and the tone more insistent, though coaxing. The volume higher, the enunciation slower as if she the listener, despite the good English, doesn't understand. Maybe I wasn't clear, where did you come from? RAT-A-TAT-TAT. How long have you been here? RAT-A-TAT-TAT.

It's the insistence she cannot abide: she is supposed to be grateful for their attention. She is supposed to meet them, all of them, more than halfway. She is supposed to be happy that they take any interest in her at all. She is supposed to thank them. They are expecting her to demonstrate how well she knows the word *obeisance*. "Over there." She points in the general direction of the nearest hospital, careful to look just past their shoulders into the expansive eyes of blue sky, into the stoic hearts of oaks or the spindly branches of pine. The houses display the American flag, when thirteen colonies declared their independence. RAT-A-TAT-TAT "Native speaker" RAT-A-TAT-TAT.

The laughter that follows is tainted with incredulity. What do you do? RAT-A-TAT-TAT You do work, yes? RAT-A-TAT-TAT RAT-A-TAT-TAT. RAT-A-TAT-TAT.

She stifles a yawn and blinks rapidly to keep her eyelids, suddenly so heavy, from closing. "Writer," she says instead of journalist. RAT-A-TAT-TAT RAT-A-TAT-TAT RAT-A-TAT-TAT RAT-A-TAT-TAT RAT-A-TAT-TAT RAT-A-TAT-TAT.

Their eyes roll as inevitably as sunsets, as low tides.

&

Maybe if she lies still, they'll grow tired of this game. Maybe the agents will grow tired and take their guns and their bullhorn and their bulletproof vests and go home.

&

Her beloved Greta arrives in the new house, after a lengthy doctor's appointment. She walks from room to room, sticks her wet nose in everything and sniffs. At the front door she waits patiently for her human mother to take her home. Seeing this, the children bound downstairs and wait with her. The girls smile and Greta pants. Unfortunately, Mother met with her real estate agent and closed on the old house the day before. A nice older couple from Kentucky and their sons live there now.

&

The agent who searches her is not the same agent who discharges his weapon. The agent who fires his assault rifle has blue eyes and a wisp of a mustache.

For the first time in years, she cannot swallow her feelings down the dark hole of her esophagus, and let them flutter like bats in the center of her stomach. For the first time in years, the act of swallowing is dangerous. What if the agent notices she's awake? Will he finish the job? She is on the driveway. If she were in a hot yoga class, this would be the corpse pose. Except that her legs are not two straight lines, her toes are not pointed.

&

Matt coughs into his closed fist. He uses the same hand to give her the assignment. She wants to douse the paper first with the sanitizing gel and then with the cigarette lighter fluid on his desk and set his office on fire.

She tries not to frown, she tries not to look directly into the city editor's crystal blue eyes.

She looks over the typed words, clipped instructions: the fortieth anniversary of JFK's death, another series of cold calls to strangers, hoping someone is old enough to re-member what they were doing the moment the president was shot. She knows how these stories go, inevitably some-one will ask her the same question, and she will have to tell the truth.

That she wasn't alive then.

Well, at least not in her present incarnation.

The City Editor is astute. "You don't have to do this as-signment, you know." Matt's tone is conversational, as if she has a choice. But the smile on his nicotine-stained lips does not reach his eyes.

Not doing the assignment is tantamount to being fired. She uses every muscle in her face to form a smile that mimes gratitude. "I look forward to it," she murmurs, and leaves the office, careful to close the door behind her.

•

She stands by the bank of desks, like a girl at a prom, waiting for someone to ask her to dance. She doesn't have to wait long. Her old buddy from j-school days swivels his chair around from his computer screen. "Come sit next to me," Chris says, pointing to the unoccupied desk across from him. "Grant is sick today."

She smiles at him and walks over, puts down her bag, plants herself on Grant's elevated seat. Grant is a fierce business reporter and can bark at the presidents of Fortune 1000 companies when he doesn't like their answers to his pointed questions. Grant has spoken to her mother-in-law before, on a number of occasions. Grant is also four-foot-eleven, with a sweet tooth for doughnuts that forces the lower buttons on his blue work shirts to pop off onto the newsroom carpet.

Chris sees the assignment sheet and holds up his own copy. "This should be riveting," he says. "Four years of j-school, a graduate degree, and bone-crushing debt have really prepared me for this moment of asking older people to relive a particularly traumatic moment from their youth."

She laughs, breathes in the smell of someone's lasagna or pizza heating up in the break-room microwave a few feet away.

Her former classmate Jess, general assignment reporter often stuck covering school board meetings and zoning board votes about mixed-use developments, pokes her head up from her seat, warms her hands around a steaming cup, presumably coffee. "I've received one of those, too."

The other business reporter on duty, Scott, strokes his

flaming red beard and readjusts his Coke-bottle frames. "Me, too," he says, his voice gravelly, tired.

Chris smiles. "Let's have fun," he says. He picks up a pack of playing cards from his desk and shuffles them expertly. The red-and-blue design on the back looks like a pagan goddess from where she sits. After a long moment, he spreads the cards out like a fan before him and asks her to pick a card.

Mother chooses a jack of diamonds.

Chris nods. "Remember it," he says and takes back the card, begins shuffling furiously. He cuts the deck several times as he spells out the reporting rules for this JFK assignment: the pages in the phone book will only be turned to sections where surnames match former presidents. "I'm buying beer later to anyone who can get an Eisenhower or a Taft," he says.

She chimes in. "We are in Georgia. No Carters unless it's Jimmy."

Scott laughs. "The copy editors are going to key our cars."

Jess sniffs. "I took the subway." That is not the name of the public metro system in Atlanta, but Jess uses the term she learned when she and the Real Thing were in New York together, for graduate school, a decade ago.

Chris pulls out the jack of diamonds from the pile and hands it to her. "Your card, right?"

•

Mother cannot understand why she is being given this assignment. She cannot ask intelligently of anyone to reexperience a traumatic moment like that. Most of the names on the potential list of businesspeople are friends of her bosses on the City Desk; the nepotism is so thick it's strangling her supply of oxygen. Inevitably the question will be asked of her, and her answer will short her credibility.

"How can you convey accurately what you haven't seen or experienced yourself?" one old woman will ask.

"Oh, that's easy," she will say, tossing her hair back like a horse's mane. "I wasn't alive during Partition, yet I see the effects and consequences of that decision every day, through the years, imprinted on everyone's faces. Everyone around me who was brown and Bengali as I was growing up. What it means to be forced to leave."

The more astute, like the gentleman who shared a last name with a president in the 1970s, but nothing else, will say, "I can say the same. The consequences of that one day in 1963 and that one man's actions changed me and my family and my community and my city and my state and my nation forever." Oscar is not on the list of who to ask. He is on the street corner at a kiosk selling cigarettes and magazines.

What she wants to do is ask this man, with the aquiline nose and russet-colored skin, where he was three years earlier, in 1960, when those students refused to relinquish their seats at the lunch counter in Greensboro. She wants to ask Oscar what he does now when they look past him at the deli checkout counter or the movie theater, when the young zit-popping punk behind the glass booth tells him all the seats are taken when he knows that they are not.

Instead she dutifully asks him personal identifying information and thanks him for taking the time. She asks his name and age and hometown, but she already knows all of these things about him.

Still she asks.

"It's always good to see you," Oscar says, this man who used to drive a city bus in small-town North Carolina and watch a little girl transfer all by herself every weekday morning, then walk, rain, sunshine, or sleet, the last half mile to school. "You're still the same."

She smiles, and shrugs.

&

Until 1997, Barbie was 38-18-24.

&

Prisoners of technology, that's what people are. Chained to their personal digital assistants, their iPods, their BlackBerry devices, and, of course, their cell phones, their smartphones, their ability to videoconference, to see each other when they really shouldn't be able to see each other. Her man of the hour, her hero, is definitely in the loop. Unfortunately, he is allergic to the cleaning solution that came with his new contacts, and he has just lost his glasses.

"I can't see," he says, stretching his hand out in the general direction of the bathroom.

She guides him to the door, but her ears are still tuned to the Sunday talk-show discussion about minority rights, voting rights, incarceration rates, mortality rates, literacy. A group of middle-aged well-educated white men talking about women and people of color.

What does it mean truly, to be invisible? Her stillness, her ability to remain calm while high-decibel insults are hurled inches from her face and ears. To pretend nothing has been said. To pretend deafness. Or her chameleon's ability to blend in, a nondescript body in a dark blouse and black jeans leaning against the pay phone at the hospital waiting room, or standing outside the courtroom's double doors or by the fire engine at the crime scene, yellow do-not-cross tape isolating one place from its larger context. To pretend the oak tree across the street's steadfast patience, to pretend paralysis. To watch but pretend blindness. Never look anyone in the eye. Or maybe restraint. Knowing her lack of reaction is the only thing keeping her alive, over and again. Knowing the first time she hits back is the last time she'll ever have the opportunity to do so.

&

"Come again?"

"She looks nothing like her license photo."

"Are you sure it's her?"

"Oh, it's her, all right." The agent laughs. "Looks like she knocked over the Krispy Kreme and ate everything in sight."

"Oh, Hollis."

&

Her mother-in-law comes to visit, notices the hair Greta has shed on the carpeting and her son's absence at the dinner table, the brigade of repairmen traipsing through the garage and basement after the lightning strike, the boxes that remain unopened from the move to suburbia. She is smartly dressed in a monogrammed Italian black pantsuit and casually wears a thick strand of glossy pearls; her caustic red nail polish and her lipstick match. She is the working mother of an only child. She runs a small Fortune 1000 company, and weaves tapestries in her spare time, some of which hang on museum walls across Europe. Her blond hair is fashioned into a beautiful chignon.

Mother is conscious suddenly of her "mom uniform": jeans, T-shirt that daughters use as a napkin after a jelly-toast breakfast, and greasy hair put up in a limp ponytail. Her mother-in-law waits until the children are finished with their meals and run off to complete their homework, carrot-cake cupcake and cream-cheese frosting in hand. "My god, you've gained weight." Mother-in-law helps herself to a cupcake, licks the frosting from her fingertips. "Why are you even looking at the dessert?"

&

The Middle Daughter enters the car after school, slams the door, hurls her book bag into the back, straps on her safety belt, all in one fluid motion as if she's been practicing this moment all day in her mind. She crosses her arms and commands, "Drive. Please. Just drive."

&

She ventures into the city. She is stopped outside the Indian grocery. An older female acquaintance she has not seen since her second child was born and she discovered she was pregnant. Again. After more than a moment's hesitation, Mother finally remembers she used to sit next to this older woman every first Tuesday of the month during book club. The acquaintance is a very smart woman, with a Ph.D. in chemistry, whose in-laws decided it would be too shameful for them to have their only son's wife work. Remembering all this about her, but not her name.

"I feel so tired just hearing about your daily routine." Uneasy laughter from the friend, her Bangla a smooth stroke of lapis on a painting of a bright sea. "I am just so grateful my children are grown."

"Surely you remember what it was like?"

"But you have so much more going on. Three kids, traveling husband, dog. My situation was a little different: one less kid and a husband who never left the city, even overnight." This woman could model face cream on TV; she resembles someone who has never experienced the true anxiety of parents who are outnumbered by their children: youthful, with perfectly pressed linen slacks and matching tunic-blouse, a smart shoulder-length haircut with dyed ebony hair to hide the gray.

"What does the dog have to do with this?" And then

she remembers: this woman's name is Shangamitra Ganga-padhay. She used to go by Sue Ganguli, but changed everything back to the original precolonized name once she hit suburbia. Each person of color pushing back against the dominant culture in her own way. The government of India was doing the same: she'd read that the Anglicization *Calcutta* was to be replaced by the precolonized pronunciation and spelling: Kolkata. "She's the only one who's consistently housebroken."

&

Apparently not. Greta, or Greta Girl since the very moment of her rescue from a shelter the decade before, defecates upstairs on the white carpet.

&

"Did he resist arrest?"

"Well, the way Doug tells it . . ." But a dog's warning bark drowns out the rest of his answer.

&

"What's their problem? Do you not go to the right country club? The right church? Do your kids not go to the right school? Or is it that they've already sensed that you're not only the last screaming liberal in Georgia but that you're also probably the last socialist left on the face of the planet? That you're actually willing to pay extra so that everybody gets to go to the doctor when they need to? You know, you have the look about you of a girl who once climbed up the side of a water tower just to paint the anarchy symbol."

Sigh. "They hate me because I leave the garage doors open too long sometimes." Mother smiles into the telephone receiver. "It's against the rules."

Emily laughs. "That is a serious infraction. They should pelt spoiled eggs at you."

"Don't give them ideas."

&

Mother hears the rain, percussion like the ocean, synchronized; cracks open one eye to be confronted by clear sky. She closes her eye again when the neighbor across the street two doors down on the left yells out "oops" and Mother hears her walk away, possibly to turn off the sprinklers that have been forbidden since the drought started years ago. The policemen are too busy at Mother's house to issue her neighbor a citation for breaking the rules.

&

Raining the day she becomes smitten with Weatherman John. Day off. It has rained for weeks without end, and it continues to rain, and the weatherman looks positively bored every time he has to deliver his soggy predictions and wretched forecasts, sound his warning bell. "I don't know why I'm even bothering," John says, pointing to another wave of storm systems moving through the Midwest, heading straight for Georgia. "Yes, it's going to rain more, and no, it will not impact our drought, because it's raining too hard. The ground is saturated as much as it can be in this drought and everything is running off, and yes, there will be more flooding, and no, there's no way to avoid it."

She is light-headed, a little dizzy, but attributes it to this new crush and not to the fact she has skipped breakfast and perhaps lunch. She cannot recall. She also can't remember how long she has been manning the house all by herself, how long her husband has been away, how much longer she'll be solo. The weatherman's pretense is gone, as well as his optimism that the sun will shine tomorrow or the next day. John tells it like it is going to be. His tone is as flat as the Midwest whence he came. There is no hope in his voice, just resignation. His acceptance of the inevitable is happiness coursing through her veins. Not only is he consistent, this weatherman who bears an uncanny resemblance to Clark Kent, glasses and all, but also he's on every night, same time, same channel. She could set her Swiss watch to this man, the Swiss watch her mother-in-law gave her for her birthday the week before, when she turned forty.

&

". . . Not like this woman here," the agent says. "Very stoic . . ."

&

"Just think of it as a game," she tells the Middle Daughter, who is crying in the backseat, because she wasn't invited to her classmate's birthday party. Everyone else came to school on Monday wearing the tie-dye T-shirt they'd made over the weekend.

"What game is that? Pick on the girl who looks different?"

Mother moves her brand-new copy of *Half a Yellow Sun* off her lap and to the passenger seat. "No, it's called Stiff Upper Lip," she says, making up some "ancient" British history along with her faux British accent. "You're actually playing it right now."

"Right, I'm losing," Middle Daughter says, wiping the tears away with her fingers.

"No, you're not," says Mother, handing her a box of tissues, "because you didn't cry in front of them all day. Right?"

Middle Daughter stops crying. "What do I win?"

Mother can't help but smile. Chip off the old block and all that. "Their respect, eventually. In the meantime, you can wallow, the way a pig wallows in mud, in the satisfaction that they won't ever see you cry over anything they did."

Middle Daughter blows her nose with a tissue. "Did this happen to you?"

Mother nods. "Can I tell Daddy now?"

"Nope."

She sighs.

&

In 1997, Mattel produced a Barbie that needed a pink wheelchair. A high school student in Tacoma pointed out the
wheelchair couldn't fit into the elevator of the Barbie Dream
House and Mattel had to redesign each dream house to ac-
commodate the chair.

&

She closes her eyes and a kaleidoscope appears, the blue of the sky giving way to the red pulse of pain near her stomach. She opens her eyes and the sky is a clean slate now, the little wisps of cloud are all but gone. The sky is the color of her alma mater: she thinks of the bumper sticker she put on her first car when she was exactly half the age she is today: *If God Isn't a Tar Heel Then Why Is the Sky Carolina Blue?* The pain is less when she doesn't give in to the light show. But the light show is hard to ignore: every time she opens or closes her eyes, the blues and blood reds are reinvented; she is witnessing the continents shifting, the tectonic plates of years shifting and crashing into each other. She spies the steeple of the neighbor's pine tree at the bottom corner of her line of sight. The owl is no longer hooting, and the neighbor with a lawn mower starts his engine. The shadow of the policeman crosses her face, and she closes her eyes, shutting them tightly as if she had never opened them at all.

&

"Why is it necessary for them to be in so many activities?" Grandmother asks, her voice tinny in the crackling phone connection. The landline always crackles when the weather is bad. "Why do you have to overdo everything you do? Why can't you just do what I did? You didn't turn out badly."

Mother grits her teeth and wills herself not to answer. She wants to tell her that growing up in the shadow of maternal depression and homesickness for India made her neither confident nor accomplished in anything except reading books. She wants to remind her that all she ever wanted to do was run—cross-country, sprints, marathons, whatever—but she couldn't convince Ma to drive her to practice, couldn't convince Baba to allow her to wear shorts in public, or buy her decent shoes that were made in America. It is a little more than a year before the agents are in her driveway.

She wants to tell her mother about the vow she takes every day never to speak to her parents again only to break it when either parent calls. She wants to express regret, she desires to practice forgiveness, and she wants to wish aloud for change. None of these things will materialize, no matter what she says, so she decides to make a game of it, she plays the girls' "Quiet Game" in her mind.

She offers herself a reward if she can just get through the next ten minutes without talking back, a trip to the bookstore, a hardback of her choice. Gandhi remained silent one day each week, and look at the change he effected: He set a nation free.

"I know what you are thinking," Grandmother says, "even if you don't have courage to say it."

Mother grins, smiles, laughs even, but silently. The receiver is covered and all either hears is static on the line.

"What's become of you? You never lacked courage before."

Sigh. Tears of laughter are unexpectedly sliding down her face but still Mother doesn't utter a sound until Grandmother abruptly hangs up.

Mother wins. Later that day she stands in front of the new-fiction shelf at the bookstore near the girls' school and sees *Beloved*, now out in the twentieth-anniversary-edition paperback. She'd missed the author's appearance the week before but there on the neighboring shelf is an autographed copy. She snatches it up and heads for the cashier.

&

She attempts to practice forgiveness every day. Most days, when she sneaks in a telephone call to her presently nonexistent sister and they've shared a giggle or two, she's successful and moves through the hours with ease, finds humor and practices smiling. Even to the people at the Middle Daughter's school. She can almost forget Greta's absence, she can almost forgive her Hero's. Sometimes, when the nonexistent sister takes a temporary vow of silence, Mother is adrift, not so lucky. Then every act is laborious: working, eating, reading, writing, cooking, driving, breathing. The Baby Sister, who is now a sister of God's, has been silent for the past month, and Mother is faltering. Nowadays, smiling is simply out of the question.

IN MEDIA RES

. . . in which she realizes her arms are beginning to tire, that the cold she's been nursing for weeks is really an allergy of the worst sort: all the things she's ever loved to eat, garden Roma tomatoes, chickpea-and-potato curry, ice cream, corn pudding, are making her stomach turn. Turn like a cluster of butterflies in the hothouse at first, and then a roller coaster, Curtis the TV news reporter beginning his report by naming her hero, and then the whirling dervish of a tornado touching down very close to her heart . . .

&

"I didn't want that for you," Grandmother says, recounting how her own natal family in India was never alone.

Too many people. Too many voices trying to speak at once, too much pollution, too much noise. Grandmother says they started out in a joint family, and although Mother knew what she meant, that Dadu's brothers and their wives and children all lived in the same house for a time, what the American-born daughter pictures is a room empty of furniture, family skeletons sitting in a circle, elbow to jaw, hip to bony hip, banana-leaf fronds for plates, steam rising from the hill of rice on each plate, cogwheel-shaped slices of fried bitter gourd on the side, waiting for someone to serve them sour red lentil soup. Too many people in one tiny space. Not enough privacy. Then she pictures the construction-paper cutouts that her first-grade teacher was good at making, faceless naked dolls all holding hands, waiting for someone to draw in their smiles, and their black-ink eyes.

"Look what I got instead," Mother says, hand stretching out like a game-show hostess over her empty living room. "A life-size dollhouse with a crazy mortgage and a husband who's never at home."

&

Her father says soon, when the Real Thing asks the first time, and soon enough by the time she asks the sixth time. It wasn't as though he had to order the bike, even. They had picked out the violet-bodied two-wheeler with matching streamers at the handlebars, and somehow shoved it into the trunk of the green Nova that Saturday. But the seat needed adjustment, and so the bike languished at the bottom of the steep driveway, in pieces, waiting to be made whole. Now Wednesday. The girls in the neighborhood, the nice ones like Leslie and Karen, let her take short rides down the street, in exchange for a turn on the future promise of the purple bike. Tammy and her horrible brother Donny laugh at first, sitting atop their bikes, zooming down the street like hall monitors, with helmets and black gloves. Donny tells her that her father is too stupid to know how to adjust the bike. Tammy smiles but the smile doesn't leave her lips and transform her unhappy face. "There are rules, you know, where someone like you can ride."

Karen starts to argue, but her mother comes to their family's front porch and calls her inside. A car with open windows cruises by, the Bee Gees blaring on the radio.

Leslie looks at Donny. "I won't go with you anymore if you talk to her like that."

154   DEVI S. LASKAR

It is fine that day and the next one hundred and twenty-seven days, until Leslie moves with her family to Charlotte, until Leslie's house with the wraparound porch is emptied of its possessions and a childless couple moves in.

&

The mustached man in navy blue asks her, "Do you know where your husband is?"

She stares at him with the look she reserves for her children, when they've bloodied each other over a toy, a dress, or a turkey and cheddar sandwich. He cannot hold her gaze. She decides he doesn't already know the answer to the question he is asking. "No," she says.

He lowers his gun from her temple so that it's pointing, roughly, at her trachea. "You're not afraid?"

Although she's still in the newspaper business, she has been out of the crime-reporting business for more than a decade. But in this moment when the man holding the gun is also wearing the bulletproof vest, she feels the hustle of the daily news deadline inside her, the telephones ringing shrill, breaking news coming over the wire, the bark of the copy editor in the distance, the unspoken demand for getting the story and getting it right. She looks at him and says nothing.

"Do you understand me?" he asks loudly. "You should have stayed in your own country."

"I'm American," she says, the sun instantly hot on her face, the sky a blue invention, the air dog-day muggy. "I am in my own country."

Another vested policeman steps toward her, warrant in hand. "I need to search you," he says. "You could be packing."

She hesitates, for a second. "No."

The agent with the assault rifle takes one step closer to her, as if it were a game of Simon Says and she had lost a turn.

&

The slats on the shutters on the outside of the house are falling out. Every morning that he is not flying to Hong Kong or Taipei or Seoul, her man of the hour goes outside to pick up the paper and walk Greta, and every morning there is a slate-colored slat or two on the walkway or front yard. It looks like the house is losing its baby teeth, only it's not as cute. No wisdom teeth sprout to take their places. She calls a handyman, who orders replacements. He tells her it will take two weeks for the shutters to be made, painted, and then substituted. She wants to believe that the almost-new neighbors will not bombard her mailbox until the repairman comes out; she wants to believe that they will give her time. But her hero snaps his fingers in front of her face, his blue T-shirt matching the color of his eyes, the color of the sky outside her kitchen window.

"Keep looking," her hero says, shuffling through papers in the kitchen. "Maybe the neighborhood covenants are in that box over there."

She checks the oven and sticks a fork in the pan. "Why are you so desperate for them, now?" It comes out clean.

"I just don't want us to get sued by the neighbors because we took too long to get them repaired."

She wonders if she can fashion a placard and hang it from the red flag on the mailbox: "Please excuse our dust!" like at the home improvement store. She wants to believe that a public apology will keep the neighbors at bay. "What are you going to do?" She tries to sound calm and reasonable. "It's out of our control."

She stuffs her hands into the red oven mitts and pulls out the pan of brownies. The smell is making her mouth water.

"Keep looking," he says, his voice distant, as if he were far away, calling home, checking in. "I have to leave soon."

The shrill repetitive cry of an ambulance in the distance.

But she turns back to the rectangle of chocolate goo, her need for chocolate so great her hands start to tremble.

&

An agent turns on the siren of his squad car, just for fun.

&

It is warm and will only get hotter, humid and will only get wetter. It is not quite mosquito season, but when the mosquitoes arrive they will be the size of swallows. The first of the heat waves has already arrived. From dawn until dusk, she will be hot and wet, her makeup will run, her hair will frizz, her T-shirt will cling to her like a new baby, she will stink like a ham sandwich that was overlooked when the doggie bag was emptied and stayed out on the kitchen counter all night long. That is, if she makes it through this moment, on her back, her face pointed in the general direction of heaven.

&

She confesses over the phone to Emily that all she really wants is for her family to leave her alone. She and Greta sit side by side on the front porch. "Not forever, not even every day. Just a few hours each week." The words tumble out of her mouth and then she closes her eyes and ears, waiting for the rebuke. The street is empty, the neighborhood kids are at school. Tides of shame and regret crash through her for a moment and then she hears the response. It takes several moments before she understands that the gurgling chirp she hears is not her ex-roommate's disgust or tears. Just her crazy maniacal laughter.

"Welcome to Earth," her former roommate says, in between gasps. "Sit down, stay awhile." She is Californian. Her sensibilities are different.

"Really?" Mother asks. "You're not disgusted?"

"For what? Wanting five minutes for yourself?" She snorts. "No." Emily invites her to visit. Alone. "There's a summer workshop. You should apply."

"Where? In California?"

"No, Mars." More laughter. "The shuttle is expensive, book now."

Mother leans into Greta, and realizes she is the problem: she cannot leave her children alone. She cannot leave Greta. She simply cannot lower the shield. The times have changed, the times have remained exactly the same, and she is the illustrated definition of *timorous*. Until they have shields of their own, functional shields made out of an intellectual version of Kevlar, she cannot send them outside to play unsupervised. Apparently she cannot even send one of them to school. It is not safe. She is their only line of defense. She is the wall, the river, the buffer. She is the only thing that stands between them and the crazy world and the crazy people and the crazy thoughts outside. She is the person in the movie who is pushing against the door while something big and wicked on the other side is trying to come in. As a journalist she's been on the other side of that door. She can hold the door closed, just until they leave for college. She can, she hopes she can. She has to, somehow. Greta will help.

&

The end of the water slide, the moment where the body is squirted off the bright blue plastic chute, is too high off the surface of the water. Not quite the end of spring in Georgia, but already high blue of summer hot on this trip to a tropical island, she and the girls at the hotel pool while her hero is in the hotel conference room at a business meeting. She doesn't remember the exact measurements she researches later at the library. She does remember the boy's name, Luke, like the protagonist in *Star Wars*. She doesn't remember what she wrote to the hotel management, or to the pool company, exactly. She knows it's too high because she is a minute or maybe two behind this action. Luke is ahead of her, his body curled into a cannonball, the boy's unexpected scream, too high-pitched—he was not shouting in celebration. The sound echoed up the tube was a warning: fear. No, that's not quite right. The end of the water slide isn't the problem exactly. It's the water. No, that's not quite right either. There's something in the water. Yes, that's right. There's something in the water, one of the underwater barriers has become unlatched, and drifted—and Luke, balled up and ready for the picture-perfect entry, crashes into metal.

&

The pain in her stomach shifts north toward her heart.

&

She reads in the newspaper today that two thirds of all Americans get their daily "servings" of vegetables from French fries, potato chips, and iceberg lettuce. She is waiting in the car line, a doughnut in hand. She also reads that the French fries and the potato chips (and the burgers they come with) are all really made from corn, that the cows slaughtered for food have been injected with antibiotics because their living conditions are so unhygienic and diseased, that most of the corn the farmers grow in these United States goes into high-fructose corn syrup, which sounds delicious but is really poisonous, and that for one dollar, one can buy 1,200 calories' worth of potato chips or 70 calories' worth of celery stalks.

She sighs, takes the last big bite of the chocolate glaze, grateful her children love celery and broccoli and zucchini. Grateful they have not yet developed the raging sweet tooth their maternal grandmother has, especially grateful they do not eat when stressed, like their mother. She looks at the clock on the dashboard; her daughter is late. Today is the worst after-school day: piano lessons, swimming lessons, karate class, tutoring in math, and a mountain of homework before the Friday pile of tests. These things—to provide structure and proficiency, to avoid the fate of their mother—present a fighting chance that when the girls grow up they will be able to avoid the most prevalent question in society today: "Would you like fries to go with that?"

The Middle Daughter gets in the car, slowly, a blood-stain the size of a silver dollar on her forehead. "The people at my table didn't like the fact that I ate the salad from the cafeteria, Mommy."

She parks the car in the emergency fire lane and smashes the hazard button; a partial chocolate fingerprint remains on the switch. "What did they do, hit you with the salad bowl? Bang your head against the table?"

School officials walk to the car and tap the passenger window, tell her through the glass she has to move. "They waited until recess and dragged me by my hair across the playground, Mommy."

She must be shooting especially vile death glares from her eyes because the officials are backing off, turning around, walking away briskly. Mother glances at her hands, relieved to find she hasn't misplaced her composure and executed a middle-finger salute. "What?"

"They wanted me to say that I didn't like salad, Mommy."

She gulps. "Did you?"

The Middle Daughter's grin was a lightning strike, it could have lit all of Buckhead for a week. For a long moment, it was her daddy's long-ago smile. "No way."

"Can I tell Daddy now?"

"No, no, no."

Mother peels away from the curb.

&

Her uncle buys her ice cream in a blue paper cup, a miniature spoon made of wood as a utensil stuck to the underbelly of the lid. The Kwality Store at the mouth of the Calcutta Zoo, the air-conditioning of the tiny shop leaking out onto the walkway and the zoo; the roll-all-over-the-ground smell of the elephants and the pacing tigers competing with the delicate tutti-frutti strawberry-banana-peach perfection on her lips. The Kwality sign painted bright yellow and red. On the neighboring wall, cheap posters for *Sholay* still plastered everywhere, though it's been four years since the Hindi movie first opened and made Amitabh Bachchan a superstar. Her uncle offers to take her again. She's seen it at least six times, and has visions of growing up and marrying Amitabh one day. "Before we get home, let's stop at my friend's place of business," her uncle says. "I'll teach you how to play gin rummy."

She offers her uncle a bite of tutti-frutti. "It's a deal."

He accepts. "Don't tell your mom."

She laughs and ice cream dribbles down her chin. "Don't tell yours, either."

&

"Ma'am, I know the sidewalk is public property, but y'all are going to have to wait on the other side of the street. We're fixing to get out the yellow tape."

&

In her dream, she is back at the Butterfly House with her hero, not too long after they return from their grand wedding in India. The fritillary garden is a hothouse, a greenhouse with clear glass cathedral ceilings, and they stand in silence, in awe, fingers entwined, taking in the cluster of monarchs and what looks like stained-glass wings, only they're alive. The telephone rings in this dream, because in the real life upon which the dream is based, the telephone really does ring, at the desk in the hallway of the annex to the hothouse. It is a shrill clanging not unlike the sound of an alarm at a firehouse, and the beautiful orange is replaced by emergency red, the red of the fire engines in the nearby station house, the red ink from her teacher Sister Joan who gave her a D in the mandatory religion class in fifth grade because she couldn't abide a non-Catholic topping the class.

ACT II:

LOW LIKE LOSING HOPE

. . . in which she finally learns the definition of *abattoir*, what it truly means; and then wants desperately to sell off her possessions in a public auction, send the girls to live with distant relations in obscure countries with regulated cable and one government news channel, then apply for a job with the butcher down the street . . .

&

She does not leave the Butterfly House in southern Georgia, exactly. She is still there, only years have passed and now the girls are present, a chain of dolls holding hands, a chain of dolls dropping hands to point, and to cover their mouths as they exclaim their joy. The monarchs are still there, and also the others with the terrific names, *Papilio ulysses* and his twilight-blue wings, *Parantica sita* and her red, black, and white combination that almost looks like a drawing. Her hero bends down to speak to the Youngest Daughter and they share a laugh. Then the telephone rings, because in this part of the dream, it still follows the real life, when the Hero's cell phone rings. He straightens up, and slides his finger across the phone screen. She raises her eyebrows at him. "Work," he mouths to her, "have to take this," and walks away, jovially greeting the person on the other end as he exits the hothouse through the annex.

Her daughter's plaintive cry for her daddy dissolves into fuchsia, the color that royalty wears in India, known as the color of queens, the color of the sash on her daughter's dress, a sash she picks at and unravels as she is left alone.

Mother's eyes are slits and the sky is a thin blue line, too light to be the skin of the figurine pantheon of Hindu gods Grandmother has brought to her house over the years, statues that she prayed to; too dark to be considered pastel blue, the blue that is worn on baby boy skin.

&

Mother opens and closes her eyes again as the broadcaster begins to speak, he is standing on the sidewalk, no doubt looking straight into the camera eye, no doubt wearing a suit, and holding a microphone. "I don't know if they'll let me go up to the front door, Curtis."

"Gotta try," the voice she presumes to be Curtis replies.

The broadcaster chuckles.

And she sees a field of sunflowers, the very ones she stopped to photograph with her hero, two summers before in California. She hears this stranger's chuckle, and remembers her hero in the stalks of the too-tall sunflowers, yellow swaying in the wind, yellow swaying to the wind chuckling as it combed the field.

&

Greta vomits yellow all over the bottom of the stairs, then retreats back behind an especially tall pile of laundry just waiting to be folded and put away. Her human mother calls the vet, and after a brief consultation, puts Greta on a rather bland diet of white rice and makes an appointment to be seen. Her hero walks in from a red-eye that bled into a breakfast business meeting at the airport. Terminal E, where all the international flights dock after landing. He surveys the landscape and drops his carry-on by the stairs. He sits down next to Greta and pets her, puts his arm around her, buries his face in her part-collie coat.

"How are the other girls?" her hero asks, his voice muffled.

"Better than Greta," she answers, "but not by much."

He doesn't reply and she looks closely to see that he's nearly asleep. She nudges him and he slowly gets up and steps past the wet carpet and upstairs to bed.

Greta throws up something at once shiny and brown. Upon closer examination, the culprit is identified: a couple of Hershey's kisses. She wonders aloud where her beloved got the poison-to-dogs chocolate, but Greta sits like the Sphinx and does not answer.

She cleans up the mess, and after throwing away the paper towels, she looks out the front window, to the street empty of neighbors and outside life, empty except for the white mailman who stops his postal truck at the mailbox across the street. It is the first time she sees a white mailman driving a route. The first time she lives in a place where no one waters their own plants or cuts their own grass.

&

She remembers her paternal grandmother's stories from the *Ramayana*, she remembers Thakur-Ma's raspy whispers when they were both supposed to be napping after lunch, how her grandmother's voice sounded like the wind rustling through trees in the backyard, how the king and queen were banished into the forest for fourteen years; how Queen Sita was kidnapped and, upon her release, forced to prove her innocence by walking through fire; how the queen, rather than walk through the fire a second time in public, begged Mother Earth to open up and swallow her whole. She remembers that her grandmother smiled when she said the queen's pleas were answered.

&

In 1997, Mattel tried to cross-advertise Barbie with Nabisco's Oreo cookies. The public pointed out that Oreo is a slur for African Americans—and forced Mattel to recall this particular campaign. Oreo dolls are now a collectors' item.

&

"Textbook execution today, fellas."

&

An advertisement appears on television most weeknights after the children are in bed. It plays on most channels, from sports to news, from classic movies to cooking. An ad for cars, with a middle-class Black family. A husband and wife, with several children, driving somewhere together. From California, Emily calls to read her an excerpt from an online newsletter which asserts that the ad is not intended to entice minority families into buying suburban vehicles, but rather to make white families feel good about themselves for being drawn to an ad that has people of color prominently featured. And, she guesses, to make them comfortable with the idea that these people will one day become their neighbors.

"Some people didn't get the memo," Emily says.

&

"Yeah, I saw the 'Beware of the Dog' sign, too. But I didn't see the dog or his water bowl or anything like that. I think it's a hoax."

&

A week after the summer drought begins her hero gets home from the airport, and she watches through the window as he goes out to the front of the house to see 1) the sickly grey-hound that belongs to the neighbors on the left in the Queen Anne–style throw up on his highly anticipated morning paper and 2) the pit bull, which lives with the neighbors on the right in the fake English Tudor, march over, unleashed, to the mailbox and lift his back leg.

Her hero, her man of the hour, runs back inside the house. "Did you see that?" he asks her.

She is standing at the sink, sluicing purple nontoxic paint from a throw blanket. There is a colander filled with peeled shrimp that still needs rinsing at her side on the counter.

"Where have you been? Their dogs go unleashed and poop in our yard since day one."

"Who made us the doggie poop palace?"

"I tried telling you but the phone connection to Kyoto really stinks."

"Shouldn't we lodge a complaint?"

"To whom?"

"Can't we do something? Did you ever find the copy of the covenants?"

She shakes her head and points with a paint-covered finger to four boxes of "Important Papers" marked as such in the kitchen. "I'd start there."

He opens the boxes with a steak knife to find *Star Wars* figurines, the Eldest Daughter's homework from the previous school year, and some manuals to kitchen appliances they left behind when they moved. "Wow."

She laughs. "Let me point out that almost every other box is marked in this way."

"Where do we go from here?"

"We don't go anywhere," she says. "I stay here to clean and cook, and you forage, with the knife, to the basement, where all the other unopened boxes are."

Still she follows him and watches from afar, so she can make a story out of it one day. While in the basement, her hero decides aloud that he doesn't like her jotting down everything he says, likes it even less that she's writing a story about him, about the kids, about their life in Southern white-sheeted suburbia. He cannot talk to her when she's working; she has forbidden it when she takes those few minutes to scribble down their stories. He decides aloud to send her an e-mail, from his smartphone. He tries many different approaches, from angry to wheedling, cranky to crying, erases each and every one, gets up from the children's miniature pink sofa, where he is Gulliver in a Lilliputian land, paces, finds the remote. He adjourns to watch television on his man-cave big screen for a few minutes, sees a political ad, gets an idea, and sits back down to compose his thought. He sends it off, and his phone expels a swishing noise. In the distance, he can hear her phone announce a message, a bell tinkling, as if another angel got its wings in *It's a Wonderful Life*.

He turns up the volume of the game, but looks down at his phone. A copy of the message scrolls across the tiny screen: "The story you are writing is not approved by the people you are writing about. This message is paid for by your family who pays your bills."

The helmeted player from his favorite team runs effortlessly into the end zone, pigskin in hand, and scores. Her hero drops the phone onto the leather cushion beside him, bounds off the couch, and runs a victory lap around the room, arms stretched over his head as if he were Sylvester Stallone in any of the later *Rocky* films; really, though, if he had to admit it even just to himself, he more closely resembles a man who is trying to surrender, but in the dark cannot find anyone with authority.

She tiptoes back upstairs and gets her phone off the charging station. She laughs at the message and startles herself with the sound of her own cackling. She sounds like Snow White's stepmother. She is glad she is nowhere near a mirror. She stares off into the block of light from the kitchen window, just above where the sandwich press is kept. She sees the next-door neighbor direct a half-dozen shabbily dressed men in hats toward the invisible line that separates her backyard from his. And then she knows, he is constructing a wall.

Separate, and not equal.

&

In 2005, a professor from the University of Bath in England published research suggesting that girls ready to cast off childhood would often harm their Barbie as a rite of passage: decapitation and placing Barbie dolls in the microwave were considered "normal."

&

Thank God the girls are at school, out of their line of sight, out of the line of gunfire. Thank God Greta is long gone and out of their line of sight, she knows Greta would have bitten them if she were alive, she would have bitten them and they would have shot her.

Her hero, her man of the hour, she's not sure about him. He is out of her line of sight, but not theirs. It is more than probable that he was not out of range of their fire.

&

She and Greta walk around the neighborhood, and Greta stops to smell the azaleas, each and every bush, pink, white, hot pink, almost purple. The sun is setting, but the day is still brightly lit, unfinished, the sun not quite on its way down. On the way back they sneak up on the girls, holding a mock "book club" meeting to help the Youngest prepare for a school skit the next day. The gazebo where they sit is open to all and empty but for them. They discuss *The Very Hungry Caterpillar*, faces serious. They each balance their own copy of the book open on their laps, for reference.

"Well, I like the book a lot because you finally have allowed me to read the book aloud to you," the Eldest says.

The Middle nods. "I like it because it's cool to put my fingers through the holes on each page," she says. "The caterpillar is a hungry girl."

The Youngest takes a deep breath. "I like it because it's a board book, and I can read it in the bathtub," she says. "I can put soap on it and nobody gets mad."

The Eldest says, "The caterpillar is actually a boy."

The Youngest puts a hand over her mouth, to stifle a scream. "No, it isn't."

The Middle nods as if she were the one to deliver the bad news.

The Eldest says, "Turn to the page with the big sun on it. See? It says it's a he."

Pages are flipped, rapidly. "Oh dear." The Youngest says, "I think Mommy always changes it to a girl."

The Eldest says, "That's good."

The Middle clamps shut her copy. "Yeah, that's better."

Mother laughs and finds a receipt in her pants pocket, uses a short pencil from the same pocket to scribble down their comments.

"Are you writing about us again?" The Eldest glares at her, and the mother is practically blinded by all that scorn.

"Uh-huh."

"Let me tell you that if you ever put this in a book, I will make little cards and stand outside the bookstore, and on the cards I will tell people not to buy your book."

Mother carefully returns the paper to her pocket. "With daughters like you, who needs critics?" She tugs on Greta's leash and they retreat.

&

She's pretty certain her sister would break her vow of silence
if she were witnessing this.

&

The federal census agency released data unexpectedly today: she lives in a nation modeling obesity. People watch too many sitcoms, spend a disproportionate amount of their money and time eating junk and fast food, cannot locate their home states or even the United States on a map, complain about the fact that historically theirs is a nation of illegal immigrants but don't want any more people of color to come in, work harder than every other industrialized nation (in number of days) for less money and less vacation time, and then waste all their resources at the emergency room since most can't afford adequate health care. It is only Tuesday. But it's the first Tuesday in November, and Barack Obama looks poised to win the presidency. She calls her presently nonexistent sister but the Mother Superior who answers the telephone says the nuns in the convent are carrying on their vows of silence longer than originally planned.

&

Her years of experience as a reporter inform the data, the instructions, what's expected of her, what she is supposed to do. What she is supposed to do is stay silent, a statue. Statue, impassive face, body stance so quiet and unobtrusive. As if she wasn't there, letting that man touch her in a way a lover might. She knows she is supposed to be thinking of the Buddha, his trials, how this moment is just that, a single moment. All she has to do is count: One Mississippi. Two Louisiana. Three Alabama. Then it'll be over and she can think of her hero, and the girls.

&

A lonely only, her hero has always wanted to emulate the TV series *The Brady Bunch*. When the third daughter is born, he says, "Look, we have half of the Brady family. We just need to produce three boys and it'll be really close."

She attempts to be patient. Shivering from the third C-section in four years and under a pile of blankets thrown over her in an attempt to raise her body temperature, she misplaces her temper. "Do you know the premise of the show?"

Her hero shakes his head.

She realizes her sharp tone has rendered him afraid. No one in the labor-and-delivery room, save them. Even the baby is taken to the nursery to warm up in a warming tray. "The lady has three girls, the man has three boys. Their respective spouses die, and they marry each other."

To say he looks crestfallen would be to say that Jacques Cousteau is fond of fish. "Oh."

September 11 is still practically new, thirteen months have inched by, and yet the general discussion these days is whether the Pledge of Allegiance should continue to carry the phrase "Under God" as in "One Nation Under God." "So, I'm set." She nods and that is that.

He never brings up *The Brady Bunch* again; in fact, he changes the channel whenever he hears the familiar theme music. Another fact: for the past eight years, he waits to see her put a bite of dinner in her mouth, chew, and swallow before he picks up his fork and starts to eat. Of course, he rarely eats with her anymore, it is hard to have dinner with your family when you're flying across the International Date Line and do not know if it is tomorrow or yesterday.

&

But instead of ice flowing down like a waterfall from her brain, it is lava. The anger bright red and so neon blue; all she can do is start to shake.

&

Perhaps she sinks into the muck of life the day she has to find an alternate dry cleaner's, the day before her man of the hour is set to board a business trip that'll take him across three continents and eight time zones, and far away from her bloated, bleeding pregnant body.

She is six months pregnant with her third, far enough to know it'll be another sweet girl. She goes to her OB every week because of the bleeding. Her doctor tells her to relax, to make her bed an island and not to leave it except to eat and pee. She laughs each time, but never promises. She laughs aloud just then, thinking of her doctor's instructions as she takes the soon to be Middle Daughter out of her rear-facing car seat and places the baby on her hip, then helps the Eldest, not yet four, out of her restraint and onto the curb.

Her usual dry cleaner's, run by a lovely Indian couple from Bombay, is closed because of a religious holiday. A holiday she should be observing, but cannot because of her chores. She takes a chance on a big operation in an adjacent shopping center, one that she notices has a fair number of patrons. She walks in with the girls, the baby in utero hanging especially low, blood trickling down the inside seam of her maternity pants, the other baby pushing aside the sling to get a better look at the world, the preschooler holding one hand while the other hand clings to a black garbage bag full of her husband's work shirts and pants, a maternity dress upon which she had spilled brown mustard and a pink denim jumper that the Eldest Daughter had somehow smeared with acrylic paint over the back, as if she'd made a snow angel wearing that jumper—without the snow, of course.

A brunette with bottled-blond streaks in her hair is behind the counter, stares at them, unmoving, as she struggles through the door. "May I help you?"

"Yes, I'm here to drop these off," Mother says.

The blonde grunts. "We're a dry cleaner, not a day care."

"Yes, I know . . . what?"

"The day care is two doors down." Her tone is cold enough to rival the icebox at home, where the pint of forbidden mint-chocolate-chip ice cream is stored.

"I'm here to drop off the clothes, not the kids," Mother says, as her eldest squeezes her hand tighter, and each of them looks at the woman's robin's-egg-blue eye shadow and bloodshot eyes.

"If you're seeking employment, you'll have to come back when John, our manager, is here."

Mother sighs as the baby grabs her earlobe and swats her tiny gold stud, the one she put in her ears for the first time in two months, to look pretty in a moment when she felt anything but. "I don't want a job. I just need to have these clothes back within twenty-four hours."

"Let me see that bag," the salesgirl says, then shuffles through the material, missing the crimson-colored maternity dress and the denim jumper. Her stare is piercing, and as they lock eyes Mother can feel her heart racing, and the baby kick. "Where did you get these?"

"They're my husband's."

The shopgirl stares. "Do you think I'm stupid?"

She clenches her jaw to keep from laughing aloud. "Why would you say something like that?"

"Where's your ring?"

She shows her the left hand, a discolored band of flesh where the ring should have been. "I'm swelling," Mother says. "I've tried to put it on but it keeps cutting off my circulation. My finger was turning blue."

The woman nods. "You should buy a fake one at Walmart, ma'am. People are going to talk."

She wants to reach over and slap the salesgirl's face, but feels her daughter's small hand in hers. She pretends the shopgirl's face is a dartboard and that her own eyes are darts. She was once a bull's-eye dart thrower, back during President Reagan's tenure, the year Orwell's dystopia predictions did not come true, when the legal drinking age was not quite twenty-one in North Carolina and she was not quite twenty-one. "That's ridiculous," she says.

"Bless your heart, I'm just concerned for you."

She looks behind the salesgirl, at the carousel of clean clothes, all wrapped in plastic, and each piece hanging neatly off its own wire hanger. "That's lovely. Please return the bag to me."

The woman rolls her eyes. "There's no need to get snippety, ma'am."

A headache forms like a funnel cloud at the back of her neck. "I need the bag back," she says, her eyes suddenly tired.

The brunette-blonde drops it back over the counter, near where she is standing. After switching the clothes to the other hand, she takes the Eldest Daughter's hand once more, and says to her, "Tell the lady goodbye."

"Goodbye, ma'am," her daughter says, waving politely.

In the car, this daughter says, "What is Daddy going to do? He needs clothes."

Mother drives and drives, the traffic signals mostly green and yellow but construction equipment like chess pawns, obstructing any clear paths. Finally a mall, in the distance, orange construction cones like a field of poppies before her—the shop signs shiny like the Emerald City. "Let's go in," the Eldest says, hope in her voice.

The next stop they make is at the department store, where they buy her hero a blazer, two new shirts, a couple pairs of trousers for work, and a new tie. The saleswoman is African American, middle-aged, with the kindest expression in her brown eyes, YVETTE printed on her plastic name tag. She coos over the baby, gives the Eldest a grape sucker shaped like a giant amethyst ring, and never asks a word about Mother's marital status.

&

She is watching herself suddenly, from the other side of the driveway.

&

Clay introduces her to a surfer whose six-pack is as shiny as his longboard. The Banzai Pipeline is at the end of its annual rage, still only the experts are out at sea.

"I can take you out," the surfer says by way of aloha. "It's safe enough."

She plants her ass on the warm white sand. "I'm just fine here."

"You?" Clay laughs. "Chicken?"

"I'm just a country girl from North Carolina." She smiles and pats the sand. "I know when I'm beat."

Clay and the surfer, whose name she doesn't catch, laugh and take off.

Clay comes back, his lion's mane and beard slicked down by the Pacific. "Howzit, Makiki Masala?"

"Warm and dry," she answers, careful not to touch her blackened eye, pushing the hair off her face. "You looked good out there."

He says, "It clears my head." A lifelong surfer.

"Walking by the water's edge does it for me," she says. "Riding the waves is above my pay grade."

Clay frowns and peers at her left eye.

"Let's go see Tommy and settle this," he says.

She stands up, brushes the sand from her pants. "My way."

"No way," he answers.

Tommy's real name in Hawaiian means "righteous." He and fifty-seven of his friends and relatives continued to occupy a famous public beach on O'ahu, not far from where she and Clay now stand. Of course, all of them stood on an island in the Pacific. Nothing was too far away. She wrote a story about Native Hawaiian rights and the Kalama family's occupation, not long after the century mark commemorating Queen Lili'uokalani's overthrow by the Americans. Clay had changed the tone of her article—less sympathetic, more adversarial—with a few choice words. But he'd left her name as the author. Tommy first yelled from the pay phone at the gas station a quarter mile from the beach where he'd been living for months. Then he'd come into the newsroom, unbeknownst to her, found her on the way to her car, and pushed her up against the stairwell. Clay had found Tommy and sent him away, and had driven her to the clinic.

A few days have passed. Now they are at the beach. "I need the follow-up story," Clay says. "I'm coming with."

"My way," she repeats, strapping on the seat belt, then rolling down the window.

"No way," he replies.

"I'm just a country girl from North Carolina," she counters. "But I do know what I'm doing."

"Not here," Clay says.

"From here to there, funny things are everywhere," she

says, quoting *One fish two fish red fish blue fish*. "I'm young, not stupid."

"Not here," he says. "My mistake."

"So you're going to be my bodyguard for the rest of my life?"

Clay smiles.

"Does Tommy go around hitting reporters?"

"I've never even heard him raise his voice," Clay says, and the surf from the ocean to their left was drowning out his words. "He's as quiet as a shadow."

The salt water sprinkles onto her shoulder. "First time for me, too," she says.

They arrive at the campsite, a shantytown of tents, tarp forts, and fires ablaze in rocky pits, the United States flag flying upside down, a sign of distress. The corrugated metal garbage cans overflow, and the flies orbit them like planets around dying suns. She thinks of her fifth-grade English teacher, and all her country wisdom. Mrs. Heath and her soft voice, and her ability to make every lesson into a work of art.

Tina, Tommy's wife and the mother to his two sons, walks up, hugs Clay. "Aloha," she says, and turns to her. "I'm sorry."

While Clay and Tina talk, she looks around and spies a mound of condiment packets near a big jug of sun tea: honey, lemon, sugar. "Do you have some glass jars?"

Tina's face, framed by the long black waves of hair, takes on a puzzle. "They're not that big."

Mrs. Heath to the rescue. "They'll do," she says. Catching literal flies with real honey, and all that the metaphor implies.

&

In 2009, Totally Tattoos Barbie came on the scene, making it possible for little girls to place tattoos on their dolls, including on their lower backs and buttocks. Parents objected to the dolls, saying their daughters wanted to get tattoos on their real bodies. In matching locations.

&

She can feel the red heat loosening her tongue, loosening her limbs.

&

Perhaps the last day the salesmen come calling in the neighborhood, their unmarked white van parked casually across the street from her, near the gazebo. Tail end of the day. Like a clown car at a circus, many forms alight from the vehicle, well dressed in a uniform costume sort of way and confidently going door-to-door despite the myriad "no solicitations" placards posted on the trunk of seemingly every tree. Presumably to sell high-speed Internet access, as the sheaf of aquamarine flyers in their hands proclaims in crimson ink.

Four from the pack break off to confront her.

Only they further divide, like insidious cells carrying disease.

One pair marches lockstep across the front yard and onto the steps, the one on the right rings the doorbell, and the one on the left uses his elbow as a crowbar as he leans in to speak to the houseguest, the daughter of a friend, and the older girls, who have answered the door. The Eldest Daughter points toward the street. The other pair draws near to Mother and Greta, who is stopping to smell a cluster of forget-me-nots near the house, her leash drawn close.

The redhead who could have been a Viking in a previous life tries to pet Greta.

A growl starts at the back of her throat, and Greta's tail stiffens.

"I wouldn't do that if I were you," Mother says as evenly as she can manage. "Greta really hates men, especially men in uniform."

He retracts his hand but does not retreat. The other one, lithe like a jaguar is lithe, who bears an uncanny resemblance to a movie star she once admired and bumped into at a grocery store before she left New York for good, smiles out of one side of his mouth. "She's either hurt or old," he says by way of greeting.

"Hurt," Mother lies, hoping it's convincing, "but on the mend."

"Let me help you get her inside the house," he offers, reaching for the leash.

"Thanks, but I'll manage," she says, trying to picture the serene face of the Buddha statue she once saw in Japan, with her hero. Instead her mind floats up Munch's *Scream*.

"We are making an offer," the Viking says, and the pair that was at her front door is now encircling her.

"I don't make those kinds of decisions," Mother says, smiling brightly at their general direction. "My husband will be home shortly." Another lie. Her hero has a flight delay and isn't due back until midnight. "You could come back later."

She gently tugs at Greta's collar, and then walks as calmly as she can to the house, entering through the open garage. She feels their eyes notice that both cars are parked side by side. She smashes the button with the palm of her hand and the door descends to its closed position—she kicks herself in her mind for having a house alarm that has been in a state of disrepair for months.

The houseguest, Carla, walks into the kitchen, where Mother is giving Greta cold scrambled egg as a reward for swallowing her peanut-butter-coated medicines. "You saw them, right? The one on my right kept telling me how pretty I am."

Mother locks eyes with this pretty girl, the daughter of old family friends, Stella and Duane, who is staying another few months until her law school fellowship runs out and she moves out west.

The Youngest runs down the stairs without uttering a word, flings open the front door, and hurls her body outside into the yard.

"What are you doing?" Mother asks, trying so hard not to yell.

"I lost the charm on Sissy's bracelet," Youngest Daughter calls out. "She said I couldn't be in her room if I don't find it."

"Not her decision," Mother replies. "Come inside."

"No!" her daughter screams. "She said I couldn't be her friend if I lost it."

Carla stays with Greta as Mother trots out the front door and into the yard. "Let's go inside to talk about it."

"No," the Youngest says, her tone emphatic. "She's mad."

The men regroup by the white van, reconfigure their strategies. She lifts her daughter's chin and stares into her eyes. "Go inside," she whispers. "Now."

"Fine," Youngest Daughter sputters, and runs back through the open door. "Mom says I don't have to! Mom says tough luck!"

Mother shows her back to the van and walks inside, closes the door, and the sound of the key turning the dead bolt soothes the sirens she hears inside her brain.

"How are we doing?" she asks loudly.

It is a train station upstairs as girls bustle and hustle from one child's room to another—the five stages of grief play out in as many minutes and then unexpected joy. Mother asks again.

"Fine," Middle Daughter chirps. "We found the charm in the bathroom."

"You might want to call the vet," Carla calls out. "Greta just threw up her meds."

Mother sighs and starts walking toward the home phone. She takes it out of its black cradle and turns it on. No dial tone. On and off a few times but the phone is dead. She tries to recall where she last left the cell phone. Perhaps in the pocket of her raincoat, hanging in the hall closet by the front door. The light shining through the patterned glass of the front door is suddenly obscured. The doorbell rings, insistent, time and again.

"Mom, make it stop!" the Eldest pleads. "It's those boys from the cul-de-sac playing Ding Dong Ditch again."

She inhales deeply and says, "Okay."

The Youngest turns on the radio, and Middle Daughter shuts the door to the Eldest's room, and Mother listens to their laughter.

At the door, these forms loom larger than seventh and eighth graders. Perhaps five, perhaps all seven from the clown van are standing on her stoop, the Viking and the actor look-alike closest to the doorbell.

She walks up to it but doesn't open it. "Yes?"

"Look, we need to talk to you," the lookalike says. "We are tired and thirsty. Can we wait inside until your husband comes home? We have an offer you won't be able to turn down."

She holds her breath for a long second. "I don't think so."

"You're lying," the Viking says. "You're just a spoiled woman with two cars and no husband."

She doesn't answer, thinks instead of the distance between her and the only object of consequence she has in her house, a fire extinguisher in the garage.

"It's not hospitable to turn someone away in this heat," the actor says.

"Let's take the door, Bill," the Viking suggests. "The cops aren't going to believe anything she says, anyway. Just look at her. She's probably the maid."

Carla's hazel eyes widen, and she starts to comb through her purse for her phone. The Mother hurriedly opens the closet door but cannot find her raincoat.

The men at the door begin shaking the handle, throwing their weight onto the etched glass, partially covered by the girls' patriotic art.

Once.

Twice.

Thrice.

On the fourth try the door hinges start to give way.

Mother puts her back against the door and pushes with all of her might. Her silent prayer is answered as Greta sprints to the foyer at top speed. She stops just short of the front door and rears up like a horse confronting a poisonous snake. Her bark is the second-loudest thing she's ever heard in her life. Greta repeatedly jumps up, her paws swatting the key in the dead bolt, snarling and barking. Her anger reverberates from the high ceiling in the adjoining living room, and it sounds like a pack of dogs are inside.

The forms step back.

Viking says, "Cujo and her spawn."

The actor replies, "Not worth the hassle for this bitch and her litter, Tom."

The band of men slowly disperses.

She slides onto the ground, her lungs out of air, her heart beating like gunfire. She turns her head toward the glass to see the forms enter the van, the actor making a three-point turn and then leaving the neighborhood. Mother crawls toward Greta, who has collapsed on the floor, and puts her arm around the convulsing body. "Good girl," she says, as she struggles to catch a breath. "Sweet girl."

The houseguest calls out, "I've got the emergency operator on the line."

"Apologize and hang up." Tears slide out of the corners of Mother's eyes. "We have to call the animal hospital first."

&

She knows a split second before she does it, that she will slap that man. Policeman or not.

&

They flip for it, and the penny is tinny as it hits the counter-top, heads up. She wins. Her stomach distended with baby, and Greta already on her leash. Night walk. Her hero wants a do-over. "Rock paper scissors," he suggests.

Rock paper scissors.

Scissors paper rock.

Paper rock scissors.

But she takes the leash and says, "You get to wheel the garbage down the hill."

In a time before cell phones. "What if you go into labor?" His face the very picture of worst-case scenario.

"Greta will bound to the rescue."

"She is hardly qualified to assist with labor."

"She has hidden talents."

He slips his feet into the leather sandals from India, a gift from his globe-trotting mother. The woman had room enough in her suitcase to bring back sandals for her son, a studded collar for the dog, and a hand-stitched gown for the baby, but strangely nothing for the mother-to-be. MIL already MIA. On another trip, planning to flow through Hartsfield for a layover the following day. Not long enough to visit, but a phone call, a hundred questions, twice as many admonitions are assured. The first grandchild is on the way, and MIL wants Mother-to-be to slow down.

"Wish me luck," he says to her as she steps out the

kitchen door onto the driveway, Greta already four steps ahead, the leash taut.

The moon is distant, a mere crescent. Street lamps buzz and hum, but neither she nor Greta bothers with anything but the walk. Feet and paws click-clacking on the asphalt. An older neighborhood, trees that stretch to the sky but no sidewalks. Greta, so thin still, eating and eating, but not yet fully healed from her litter, and the forced starvation at the hands of her previous master. Greta afraid to go downstairs to the basement, Greta afraid of all manner of belts and big white deliverymen in brown uniforms. Greta rescued but her litter nowhere to be found. She and the vet combing through area shelters, pet stores, private adoption farms for puppies. Cute German shepherd puppies would be quickly scooped up. But no one had seen or heard of Greta's puppies. Nothing. Zero. Zip.

And not a peep out of her so far. No bark. No noise at all. Ghost of a dog that eats six times a day like a puppy.

Greta stopping to smell every flower, even in the dark. Though the buds closed up shop for the evening, Greta is undeterred, sticking her nose in every rosebush, but careful to avoid the thorns. Ahead, a long slow hill and then a plateau. A little out of breath. Greta panting, too, in the humidity, the air a thick soft wall to push through. "Let's go to the cul-de-sac," Mother-to-be says, and Greta seems to nod, but doesn't pick up her pace.

They reach the crest of the hill, and as it levels off, there is the muffled cry of a man who has lost control. The front porch light glows in the distance. There is the gallop of an unleashed dog nearing and nearing closer still. Duchess, the other grown shepherd in the neighborhood. She is coming, full speed. Mother-to-be places one hand over her stomach and braces for the impact of the inevitable collision. Mother-to-be can hear Duchess bark and her master, Ian Something-or-other, start to run across his lawn in vain pursuit, his shoes making the grass crackle with each step.

Duchess gains, and she is only seconds away from impact. Mother-to-be steels herself. And then Greta hurls thunder and lightning from her throat, her barks fierce and loud and in quick succession. Duchess stops short at the curb where the green lawn stops and the asphalt begins.

And Greta bares her teeth.

Mother-to-be smiles.

The master catches up and assumes Duchess's leash. "Sorry," Ian pants.

Mother-to-be pays no attention to the man. "You can talk!" she repeats again and again to Greta.

&

The side of his shaved cheek is smooth, and his eyes register surprise as her palm lands just north of his jawbone.

&

From late-night television, her hero takes an interest in architecture and magic. On a paper towel he snatches from the kitchen, he sketches out a plan, and forages for supplies. What he wants to create is a monumental house of cards, he says aloud. Something built with his own hands, something he can make disappear. She writes down everything he says, every action. Into her blue composition book. He decides that this is how he will break into late-night television and then somehow steal the show with his wit and wisdom, his charm. She writes that his good looks are starting to crack with age, but can be hidden with powerful stage makeup. They agree that his travel schedule needs to be curtailed somehow, the girls are growing up without him.

He starts slowly at first, but soon is using all fifty-two cards in his daughters' Princesses of the World deck, cartoon smiles facing out. He builds a small castle one night after everyone is in bed and only the tree swallows and crickets are outside composing songs. He gets an idea and buys another double pack of cards on his way home from the gym, and ends up building a modern rendition of Cinderella's castle, big enough for the daughters' dolls to live in. It's a two-and-a-half-pack creation that rests on the dining room table.

He unveils the castle to his family the third morning. The children and wife look at him with great admiration, congratulate him on the dollhouse made from shiny red game cards. Just then, the telephone rings and there is the insistent sound of the doorbell. Greta runs to the door, knocking the Youngest into the Middle into the Eldest into their mother, and Mother brushes up against the table and shakes the foundation so the house collapses into a pile of pictures of pretty princesses of the world.

The telephone continues to ring, the doorbell continues its chime, the family collectively says "Oh, no!" to one another, and only Greta runs back and forth, sensing the anxiety in their voices.

&

A month after an actress bumps her head on the ski slopes and dies, Mother has been suspended from the newspaper for two weeks—for pointing out what others refuse to acknowledge, the burning crosses she sometimes sees in the distance, when she's driving on less-traveled highways. She is being suspended because she wants to write a story about the Klan rallies in North Georgia, and the city editor, Matt, said no three times, and warned her if he had to say no a fourth time there'd be no turning back. Mother couldn't help herself, kept asking to go, and she was sent home. Two weeks.

The school nurse calls and says the Middle Daughter's weeping is inconsolable. "She fell backwards on the blacktop after lunch," Nurse Angela says, her Southern drawl lengthening each word into a horrid parabola of enunciation. "But she won't tell me anything else."

"May I talk to her?" Mother asks, cradling the telephone as she sits down in front of her laptop and relays the information to her hero in e-mail form before he boards a flight home.

"Well, to tell you the truth, her teacher brought her in here, and after about ten minutes told her she had had enough and just took her back to the classroom." Angela laughs nervously. "I'm sure you understand."

Mother doesn't. "Is she bleeding?"

"No. There's a tiny bump on her head, but it's really not serious," Nurse Angela says.

"I'm sure you understand that I might feel anxious," Mother says in her best reporter voice. "Maybe I could come and get her? Take her to the pediatrician?"

"Bless your heart, I don't think you'll be able to get her now," the nurse says. "They're too close to the end of the day. Remember, today is early dismissal anyway. Just wait."

She cannot. "Her teacher took her back to the classroom, even though she was crying?"

"Well, yes, I mean, she was calming down . . ."

She hangs up, crates Greta, texts the new houseguest, grabs her keys, and runs to the car.

Mother is in the examination room with Middle Daughter and the emergency room doctor. She is wearing a Mickey Mouse sweatshirt that at one time belonged to her presently nonexistent sister, her hair pulled into a tangled bun, her leggings stained from cleaning out vomit from Greta's food and water bowls. She smells of shepherd. After a five-hour wait, the daughter's cries have subsided into a whimper.

"I want a thorough test," Mother says. "Check everything."

The doctor looks like a very young version of Dolly Parton. Her voice is as soft as a down quilt. "Kids get headaches, Mom. Kids cry about their headaches, too."

Mother points to her daughter. "This kid doesn't complain. So for her to cry means it really hurts."

Doctor Dolly's smile is sympathetic. "Of course you know your daughter better than I do, but maybe this is embarrassment on her part."

Mother makes her hands into a pair of perfectly formed boxing fists. "No, I don't think so."

"Anyway, getting an MRI exposes the child to radiation," Dr. Dolly says.

Mother stares at her, unable to prevent her lower jaw from slacking. "No more than going to get your teeth X-rayed at the dentist's," she counters.

Dr. Dolly's grin is a grimace. "Who told you that?"

"My cousin the cardiologist," Mother says. "My other cousin, the brain surgeon."

The doctor laughs. "Well, let me look her over," she says, and takes the glasses off Middle Daughter's face. "Mom, did you know her eye wanders?"

Mother responds with the magic words: "Yes, esotropia since the age of three." The spectacles are not to correct vision but to help with alignment, to prevent crossing.

Dr. Dolly sits up straight in her chair, looks over at Mother. "What do you do, Mom?"

Mother's smile is thin. "Oh, I'm the family maid and chauffeur and concierge right now, but once upon a time I used to be a journalist."

Just then her man of the hour enters the room, his suit as wrinkled as his haggard expression.

"And what do you do, Dad?" Dr. Dolly asks, as she uses an instrument to stare into their daughter's ear.

He takes out his wallet and hands her his business card.

"Thank you," she says, and takes a second to read. She reaches for the telephone instead of a stethoscope. "I have a child here who needs an MRI, right away."

Middle Daughter is wheeled out. Her parents start to follow, but Dr. Dolly stops them. "I didn't want to say anything in front of your girl, but she's got some bruises on her upper arm. And the scar on her forehead, right at the hairline. You know anything about it?"

Her hero gasps. "What? What are you saying?"

Mother blurts out, "A couple of boys at her school are bullying her." Then she clasps a hand over her own mouth. "I'm supposed to keep it a secret."

"From whom?" her hero asks.

"Which school?" the doctor asks.

Mother and her hero say the name in unison.

The doctor nods. "I went there, for high school. Those folks are old money, they're not going to lift a finger."

Concussion. Weekly trips to the neurologist and neuro-ophthalmologist for the coming six months plotted like graph theory on the wall calendar in the kitchen. Mother's comments scathing as she writes her daughter's letter of withdrawal.

Her man of the hour waits until she is finished, then snatches the paper from her, folds it into a sleek jet, and it sails across the length of the kitchen, landing close to the garbage pail. "No."

"Why not? They need to know . . ."

Her hero shakes his head. "We have to live here."

"So? So what? You want nothing?"

"Withdrawal, yes." He folds his hands in front of him. Namaste. "Commentary from the peanut gallery, no."

"I'm hardly the peanut . . ."

"It's the gracious thing to do."

The distance is short but the drive is long, traffic is interminable. On the sports radio channel, the pundits are still debating foot faults and line judges and the African American tennis player's denim tennis skirt, years after the bad calls have been archived for history and the tennis player was awarded the loss. It is some sort of remembrance day.

Mother giggles as she reads the bumper stickers on the cars ahead of her as they inch bumper-to-bumper to the next doctor's appointment. She is behind an ancient white Plymouth Valiant and cannot help herself as she reads: "Remember, life is an epic poem, not a sentence."

Middle Daughter awakens from her nap in the back. "I told you not to tell Daddy," she says, her voice sleepy.

"Yes," Mother says, turning down the volume.

"Why did you?" Middle Daughter rubs her eyes and looks out the window to the terriers in the backseat of a yellow Fiat, stuck in the next lane.

"It was an accident," Mother says. "You were being wheeled into X-ray." What she notices is the sea of red brake lights, a sea of little Cyclops, danger.

"You got scared?"

"Yes."

Middle stretches her arms and adjusts her glasses. "I get scared too."

"I know, sweets," she says. "I wish we could be happy, and not scared."

"Poor us, Mommy," she says, and closes her eyes again. "We both lost the Stiff Upper Lip game after all."

Mother turns the knob to another station and turns up the volume.

On public radio, an interview with the most celebrated travel writer of her time, who has no use for a smartphone or a tablet, who wastes no time on social media, who lives so remotely that he must travel by train and bus forty-five minutes one way when he has to send a fax. He advocates meditation instead of travel, he advocates stellar observation instead of watching TV. He advocates exercise, such as tennis.

"What do you do when you get a good idea during a tennis match?" the interviewer asks, her tone melodious, amused.

"I stop the match," he says. "I run to the side and pull out my notebook, and write down my ideas."

She tries to speak it softly, lips barely moving, just under her shallow breath so that it almost sounds like a whisper.

It is near-silent chanting. A giggle escapes over stopping a tennis match to write down an idea; what she really wants is to blubber into a glass of vodka with ice and lime. Drinking, well, drinking is completely out of bounds: spirits create revolution on her face, blisters and hives erupt, painkillers are summoned. A recumbent cycle that does not lead to weight loss or peace.

&

And then the shot is fired.

&

In 1963, Mattel offered a *How to Lose Weight* book with the Barbie Baby-Sits ensemble. The book advised: "Don't eat."

&

She cuts their shiny hair. Thirteen colonies of lice have lingered on: mud-colored soaps and foul-smelling shampoos and concoctions of rubbing alcohol and mouthwash are no longer effective.

At the moment that Mother hacks off their braids, her own parents and her in-laws are crossing the International Date Line together, her presently nonexistent sister is celebrating Christmas with her Mother Superior, her man of the hour is at the gym on a borrowed pass before he is set to fly the next day to China. The girls weep and scream and hold their braids in their hands while their mother holds the red-handled scissors in hers.

Mother doesn't cry but bleeds as though she is having a miscarriage, blood gushing out of her though medically it isn't possible. Not possible but there it is, a bright gift that keeps giving.

&

The women in the neighborhood stop chatting, the owl hoots and then no longer hoots.

&

Perhaps the first time the Real Thing tries to fill out census data for the federal Department of Education. Coincidentally, it is the last week of school before the summer break and she knows many of the teachers will not be returning to teach in the fall, she had heard whispers, but no one has confirmed who is leaving and who is staying.

At the start of the exercise, the physical education teacher Mr. King did not want to hand her the same questionnaire as her peers, saying, "Well, I'm not sure you're supposed to get this form. It's only for Americans." He looks over the Real Thing's mother-approved kurti top and matching pants and asks, "Were you born here?"

The Real Thing says yes but doesn't add how she hopes he returns to Kentucky or Tennessee or wherever he's from, as soon as the school year is over.

The fifth-grade English teacher, Mrs. Heath, standing in the doorway of the classroom, clears her throat. "Everyone gets the same form, David," she calls out.

Mr. King reluctantly hands her the form.

The questions appear easy enough, but there are not enough answers to go around. All of the other kids in the combined fourth- and fifth-grade language arts classroom have boxes to check. Even Henry.

There are four boxed answers: White, Black, Hispanic, American Indian. There are several similar questions about citizenship asked in different ways. The Real Thing hears the roar of a plane overhead but sees nothing as she looks out the window, past the brick wall and up to the cloudless sky.

She stands up and approaches Mr. King at the head of the classroom. He smiles and points to the last box. "That's where you make a check mark," he says.

"I'm Indian American, not American Indian," she says.

Mr. Hill scratches his muttonchop sideburns and readjusts his glasses. "Oh."

Mrs. Heath marches into the room, clipboard in hand. "I can take it from here, David."

The Real Thing trots back to her desk.

Mrs. Heath claps her hand against the clipboard. "May I have your attention, please?" Everyone suspends his or her No. 2 pencil in midair and watches Mrs. Heath turn her back to the class. She writes the word AMERICAN with blue chalk on the muted green chalkboard. She takes the red chalk from the aluminum sill and underlines the word. She turns around and asks all of the students to turn to the bottom of the next page.

There is a box marked Other. And there are a few lines of space for Explanation.

The Real Thing and Mrs. Heath lock eyes.

"You are not obligated, ever, to answer these questions," Mrs. Heath says. "You have a second option: You can check Other on the second page and write the word I wrote on the board next to Explanation, and we can move on with our day."

The Real Thing looks away first, before Mrs. Heath notices there are tears starting to form at the corners of her eyes.

All the kids but Mary-Margaret Anne and two fourth-grade boys sitting behind her hurriedly check the box, write in the word, and rush to the front, where Mrs. Heath waits with a large envelope.

The Real Thing waits in line to turn in her form, blinking furiously.

"I won't always be here," Mrs. Heath says to the class as she accepts the Real Thing's paper. "But I hope you'll remember today."

&

And her stomach begins to ache. Not an ache of hunger. But an ache of loneliness.

&

Mrs. Williams, Henry's mother Mrs. Williams, doesn't like to come inside the front doors of the school. She is not like Noland's mother Mrs. Williams. Noland who has hair the color of organic carrots. Noland who picks his nose and cries when Mrs. Heath scolds him for his messy penmanship. Henry's mother Mrs. Williams prefers to stand on the sidewalk, and wait for Sister Joan or Sister Grace to finish their tasks inside the principal's office and speak with her. Henry with the perfect scores, Henry who never says a word, Henry who remains the only Black boy in the school. And she, the Real Thing, is the only girl with brown skin today. Baby Sister wouldn't matriculate to this campus for another four months.

Still Mrs. Williams gets the phone calls from the office; and Mrs. Williams shows up, standing in a black print skirt and sandals, on a sidewalk bleached white by the sun. The school's front doors swing open and shut as the other students stream past Mrs. Williams and Sister Grace that Wednesday morning. She knows it's a Wednesday because it's the day they have indoor PE followed by choir rehearsal. As if the stinky gym could be transformed by taking a white sheet off the mahogany-colored piano on the small wooden stage. The Real Thing is waiting to see what the charge is this day. She was absent the day before, with a cold. She has heard that Henry had finished his geography test, placed it facedown on his desk. And then gone to the globe, to look at Africa gleaming gold on the sphere on Mr. Hill's desk. Mr. Hill tore the paper in two unequal pieces and sent Henry to the office.

The door opens and Mary-Margaret Anne and her friend Ellen scoot by and she sees Mrs. Williams hold up both pieces. "He wasn't cheating . . ." Mrs. Williams says.

The Real Thing knows that tone of voice. It's the one her own mother uses when the grocer tries to shortchange her after she buys a bitter gourd from the Hillsborough produce market.

"Come inside, Deborah," Sister Joan calls out from the threshold of the front office.

Her name isn't Deborah but Sister Joan refuses to learn her real name.

Sister Joan says the Real Thing should just answer to Deborah.

It would be easier.

For everyone.

The Real Thing ignores Sister Joan. She watches Mrs. Williams mouth the words *please* and *my son*.

To no avail.

Henry is suspended.

A note placed on his permanent record, branding him a cheat.

&

She lies on the carpet of concrete on her driveway. For a single clear moment, she hears the boredom of the policeman as he grapples with her full name from her driver's license and, in amateur fashion, butchers it. "Sweet Jesus," he says into his microphone. "What the hell were her parents thinking?"

The dispatcher's mic squawks, and there is laughter. "Just spell it."

&

The Real Thing is young enough that she doesn't hear the cars on the overpass. Of course she sees them, queued up during rush hour, waiting for the light to change. She is in the backseat of the car, in a time when seat belts were definitely optional and motorists followed the speed limit. The Real Thing peeks through the space between the driver's and shotgun seat and admires the shiny chrome of the sports car in front of their dad's mint-green Nova. Their dad at the wheel. How many things she thought are muted but are actually in full force, their dad cursing in Bangla at the man in the station wagon cutting him off, their mother cautioning him to slow down, to stop swearing regardless of which language he chose, the radio playing "Midnight Train to Georgia," which their one friend from school liked and sang during recess, the car horns blaring when the driver in the turn lane doesn't bolt at the first sighting of the green turn arrow, the Baby Sister's mouth open, breathing in nap sleep, her nose full and whistling with every exhalation.

&

She lies on the concrete, wanting to laugh but can't, but the corners of her mouth turn upward. *Gift from God* echoes inside her. Her name means "Gift from God."

&

Groaning machines exhale steam behind him, hot fog lapping the countertop where canvas bags of dirty laundry wait to be dry-cleaned and made anew. Mr. Patel rakes his thin hands through his thinning hair. They look around the rest of the shop, broken glass underfoot and glistening in the midday sun. September 12. Despite the floor-to-ceiling American flag broadly displayed in the now destroyed plate-glass window. Despite the banner proclaiming "God Bless America" for all to see, they will never pass for American. A broad white man parks his German convertible in the loading-and-unloading-only zone, stomps in, sporting a keg-sized gut and aviator sunglasses.

Without hesitation, Mr. Patel greets his customer. "Mr. Jackson, thank you for coming." A smile begins its long journey from the lips to the cheeks.

Mr. Jackson grunts. "My wife said to leave it alone, but I told Missy I had to be ready the next time I got called into work."

Mr. Patel turns his back and walks into the fog, disappears.

Mr. Jackson stares straight ahead, his right hand jangling his car keys. It sounds like a dinner bell, but it is only noon. He will not look at Mother's face, he will not acknowledge Mother's very pregnant body.

Mr. Patel reemerging, with three starched button-down shirts, Oxford blue, and two pairs of khaki trousers, pressed sharply as if cut with a knife. All wrapped in plastic. The reflection from the American flag casting a red-and-white-striped sheen over the plastic and everyone's faces.

"Here you go, sir," he says, his voice calm amid the broken glass.

"I'll come back later," Mr. Jackson says in lieu of thank you, snatching the hangers from Mr. Patel's hand. "Missy's got the checkbook. Like she's going to be able to buy anything today."

"The grocery store in Marietta is open until two o'clock," Mother finds herself saying aloud.

Mr. Jackson turns toward her. "Where are you from?"

She opens her mouth.

But Mr. Jackson rushes in to answer his own question. "It doesn't matter. You need to get on home, girl."

Mother puts her hand on her distended stomach, the baby kicking. The due date is weeks away, and the airports are shut down. She must remain calm and free of labor before Grandmother can fly down to help. She cannot have a baby today. She looks over at Mr. Patel, *God Bless America* reflecting in his watery eyes. She digs the fingers of her free hand into the bundle of keys on the counter, and uses the other hand to smooth her pink maternity blouse over her stomach. "I am home," she says as softly as she can.

Mr. Patel's head barely shakes a frightened no.

Mr. Jackson grunts and walks back to his car, unlocks

the trunk using his remote. He lays the plastic-enclosed clothes down carefully.

Mr. Patel reaches below the counter and places a couple of cheap American flag stickers on the counter, near her hand. "You need this," he says, pushing it toward her. "It'll help."

Mr. Jackson closes the trunk and quickly enters his car, presses the gas, and squeals away from the curb, exhaust smoke curling in the air.

She pushes them back toward him. "Not at my house," she says.

"Please take it," Mr. Patel says. "Just one for you, then."

Mother goes home and finds her hero perched on the arm of the couch, unable to stay seated for long, unable to stand for long, his eyes never leaving the screen, the towers in an endless cycle of crumbling and then standing upright as an airplane flies into one of them, and then crumbling again.

"Mr. Patel says we should put flag stickers on our cars." She takes the sticker out of her handbag.

"We're American," her hero says, waving her sentence away as if it were a mosquito.

She holds it out to him. "No one can tell when I'm driving."

He stops, sits, stands up. "I am not going to," he says.

"You don't have to," she whispers, tucks the sticker back in her bag, and points at his dirty blond hair turning gray. "But I have to."

He punches the throw pillow, blue with tiny red flowers embroidered at the edges, with his tight fist. "You shouldn't have to prove anything," her hero says. "This is not the America I know, this is not the America I recognize."

The baby kicks. She looks at the screen, after the towers have crumbled, survivors covered in white ash and dust walking away, and she touches her stomach.

&

Perhaps it is the spectacle of Mother Nature. The special science field trip in the eleventh grade, on the very day her sister misses school because of food poisoning (someone had laced the brownies with Ex-Lax at the neighborhood picnic the afternoon before). A moment of unparalleled beauty. Their physics teacher consults the newspaper, puts sixty of his students on the yellow school bus, finds his driver's cap. After lunch on a given Monday they are driven for an hour to a particular field of tall grass just outside Greensboro. Like a master magician, he pulls out sixty special Mylar glasses from a black canvas bag. His students use the special devices to track the moon as it crosses over the sun, the last lunar eclipse in the late twentieth century. Even without the glasses, she knows something is happening: as the sky darkens, the birds fall quiet and the air takes on a strange stillness, a second midnight. It is as if each of the clocks in the world folds hands together.

Namaste.

The divine light in me sees the divine light in you.

Several minutes later as light returns, the birds make a furious noise, heralding the day for a second time. Then a whole swarm of them abandon their trees by the edges of the field and fly away. She is sixteen, and almost believes she will never again see anything quite so beautiful.

&

Mother stares at the policewoman through dark sunglasses, and watches her lips purse and then give birth to a frown. "It's for my safety," the young officer says, pulling out the cuffs. They are standing face-to-face in front of the entrance to the newspaper where Mother chronicles the dead.

She pauses a second. "You're going to arrest me for wearing shades?"

The policewoman shakes her head slightly, and a strand of mouse-brown hair escapes the untidy bun at the nape of her neck. "Stop playing. You know why I'm here."

She did not. "I'm going to be late for work."

Another officer, a tall, slim man with hair shorn close to his pink head, turns the corner and reaches the two of them—several people glide in and out using the sliding glass doors of the news building and glance at the scene before walking away. She knows none of them, and wishes she could call Editor Dennis.

"You work in there?" The policewoman laughs. "That's rich."

Her partner pulls out a flyer from his coat pocket and unfolds it. "You're wanted on three counts of solicitation, and one count of forgery."

The muscles in Mother's face try to rearrange to form a grin, but she knows that humor will not solve this problem, that to laugh would cause them embarrassment, that to laugh would put her own life in danger. "Are you sure?"

"Well, you're Angela Wallace, aren't you?" The police-woman slaps the cuffs against her own palm.

"No," she says as calmly as she can, and pronounces her full name slowly. She looks at the partner. "I have my license in my purse."

The policewoman stares. "I'm not falling for this again. You're probably carrying."

She sighs. "May I see the flyer?"

Her editor's girlfriend, Lynette, walks out of the building for a smoke.

The policeman turns it toward his partner. On the flyer is a poor-quality color photograph of a dark-skinned woman in an orange jumpsuit, her hazel eyes dead, her skin severely freckled. The only thing Mother has in common with the woman in the picture is the haircut, the feathers and layers.

The partner barks, "Take off your sunglasses, girl."

She takes off her glasses and holds them in the same hand as her car keys.

Lynette leans in for a look at the flyer. "Are you kidding me?"

Z IS FOR ZENITH

. . . in which she teaches herself to make a fist and then with her free hand, thumb through the pages of her dog-eared paperback copy of *Siddhartha*. Metaphorically speaking . . .

&

After prolonged goodbyes, the girls reluctantly allow her hero to drive them to school. He will join later, at the vet's. Mother takes Greta on her last walk, past the forget-me-nots and late summer roses, to a meadow of wildflowers, one of the last few left unspoiled in the county. The sun rises like a bullet train on schedule. They take a good many steps inside the boundary to take it in, raw life sashaying red, indigo, and orange; bees practicing scales in the trees on the edge of the field; birds flying in formation as they journey on the super wind highway; butterfly bombardiers, nose-diving into the variable blooms. A cabbage butterfly lands on Greta's nose, and for the first time in ages, Mother closes her eyes and smiles.

BRAVE NEW ORDINARY WORLD

. . . in which she stops to see an extended family of geese flying atop the tree line. The hunters' guns go off in the distance, the hunters' horses are re-creating with their synchronized hooves the thunderous heralding before the end-all squall. The dogs are closing in, and she hears a man's voice call out from behind her, "It won't be long now." She is startled awake by the tapping of her shoulder by the red-shirted flight attendant who has Greek blue eyes, asking her to put her seat upright and check her seat belt, in preparation for landing . . .

&

She is flying, the air is cool but starting to heat up as she gains speed. She circles the globe so quickly, looks in on her favorite uncle outside Kolkata just sitting down to a cup of tea, mosquitoes hovering just out of range of the incense sticks burning at the religious altar a few feet away, the faces of her maternal grandparents and great-grandparents unsmiling as they peer from their place among the mantel photographs, dots of sandalwood paste ringing each pane of glass—denoting their passage to the next life.

She is flying and visits the Taj Mahal at night, circling the marble wonder under the light of a pearly moon. An older couple on a bench enjoy the wonder of the world, and she smiles to see her parents sitting side by side.

She is flying and sees her sister in church, listening to morning mass, her face calm, her eyes clear, crow's-feet beginning to form at the corners of her almond-shaped eyes.

She is flying through time and space and at once in the newsroom sitting at her desk watching her editor yell into the telephone and then stagger to the bathroom to cry.

She is flying and then she is picking up the Middle Daughter from her former school, consoling her for the classmates' hate. She is flying and taking that daughter to the emergency room, and much later to the soccer supply store, for a brand-new jersey when she makes the team.

She is flying but getting pulled over for failing to yield at a stop sign that was removed years before, but not losing her dignity as she accepts the citation.

She is flying and walking her beloved Greta for the first time after the rescue from the shelter, on the sidewalk near her old house; Greta stopping to sniff every bluish hydrangea, every fire hydrant, and every cluster of daffodils at the base of street signposts. Greta, emaciated from neglect but swallowing medicine-laced scrambled eggs without complaint, and living another eleven years.

She is flying and Clay is smiling and handing her a spatula and telling her to cut herself the biggest slice of her own goodbye cake, since she is leaving that newsroom and the islands for graduate school.

She is flying and running as fast as she can through the new house, and this time she has caught the Youngest as she bungee jumps off the couch, this time she is successful and gives that sweet girl an extra hug, and later brushes her hair as the Youngest reads aloud *The Very Hungry Caterpillar* in her soft earnest voice.

She is flying and bringing home her first child from the hospital, swaddled in a pink blanket and hat, smiling through the pain from emergency surgery, smiling that after eight years of trying she has a baby to bring home.

She is flying and watching the Eldest flit across the stage at the civic center, a graceful and poised ballerina—the sequins from her costume glisten like stars.

She is flying and she sees each of her daughters take their first steps, and say their first No!

She is flying and she and her hero are at the park and she is watching her hero push each of the girls on the swings, and then he puts them on the merry-go-round.

She is flying and seeing herself, a red-gold bride doll, sit next to her hero, in front of a priest, red thread joining their hands as they marry. Their parents beaming for the cameras.

She is flying and she sees Henry doodling in the margins of his science notebook, and she marvels at how shiny the copper is in his penny loafers.

She knows she is still on the driveway, but there she is too, hovering in the doorway to the music room, watching the children take their places on the mini-stage, her girls in matching pink blouses and headbands assuming their positions, smiling at each other. She sees they are looking for her, and for their dad, and she is grateful and calm as the lights are brightened on the stage and lowered for the audience, as if in a movie hall just before the show is set to start. She waits for the teacher to wave her baton, like a conductor, and then she hears their voices—pitch perfect. On key.

"We've Got the Whole World in Our Hands."

Someone closes the door midway through the second refrain and she is back on the concrete.

She is flying and sees her parents at the breakfast table of her childhood, green plastic tablecloth covering the wood, everyone's faces crease-free.

She is flying and then walking Greta the last time in that nearby field, the sun shining warmly, and butterflies floating without flight plans.

&

She is flying and then she is not. She opens her eyes, sticky
with sleep. The sky looms blurry blue and the driveway pave-
ment is already warm to the touch. A tornado near her chest
sucks out the oxygen from her lungs, making it harder and
harder to breathe. Her body stops its tingling at the pelvic
bone, she is rendered a clothed, unmoving torso. Still the
keys are cold in her hand. Her phone ringing near her ears.
Special wind-chimes ringtone: her hero calling. He is alive.
She wants to answer the phone but finds that she cannot. She
has never been so thirsty as she is now, as if her mouth has
been pulled into a vacuum of sand. The cicadas resume their
patterned chirping after the shock of the shot wears off. The
trees in the backyard rustle and she imagines the owl turning
in for a good day's sleep. The women in the neighborhood are
disappearing; rather their laughter, from the moment before
the bullet leaves its chamber, is muted. She hears a dog's bark
grow sharper and louder with each second. Greta bound-
ing toward home. But that cannot be. The agents' voices are
muted and their bodies are just out of her vision though one
agent's shadow dances on her chest.

The dispatcher on the radio repeating that her hero has
been released and is on his way home.

"Copy that," one policeman says, his voice dispassionate
as if he were reading aloud an entry from an encyclopedia,
or from the pages of a telephone book.

The dispatcher drawls: "The ambulance is a minute out, Hollis."

The shadow passes over her face like an eclipse. Its voice says, "It won't be long now."

ACKNOWLEDGMENTS

Namaste for your love & encouragement. I am inspired by your fearlessness & buoyed by your friendships.

Many thanks to my agent Reiko Davis & to Meredith Kaffel Simonoff & Adam Schear at DeFiore. Many thanks to Counterpoint Press for embracing this experiment & for inviting me in to their family: my editor Jennifer Alton, and Lena Moses-Schmitt, Megan Fishmann, Miyako Singer, Yuki Tominaga, Jennifer Abel Kovitz, Dory Athey, Hope Levy, Katie Boland, Olenka Burgess, Kelli Adams, Sarah Brody, Nicole Caputo, Elizabeth Yaffe, Wah-Ming Chang, John McGhee, Ian Gibbs, Dan Smetanka & Jack Shoemaker. Special Mahalo to Jane Vandenburgh. Many thanks to Little, Brown UK & Fleet, Ursula Doyle & Rhiannon Smith & the many folks who championed this book across the pond.

My gratitude to the sea of storytellers with whom I've had

the pleasure of journeying: please forgive me if some of your names have escaped my memory. Mahalo (in no particular order): My wonderful friends at the Book Writing World, and especially the early birds who sifted through the sand with me: Jan Nussbaum, Maureen Fan, Robert Ward, Bree LeMaire, Julie Rappaport, Jacqueline Luckett, Felicia Ward, Claudia Royal, Lea Page, Sabina Khan-Ibarra, Janet Thornburg, Melanie Lee, Thais Derich, David Woolbright, Vijaya Nagarajan. Thanks to Emily Fernandez, Molly Fisk, Lise Goett, Ashaki Jackson, Wendy C. Ortiz, Ruth LeFaive, Nina Rota, Leila Sinclaire; and thanks to all of Las Lunas Locas. Many thanks to my friends from Under the Volcano, a special shout-out to the 2013 food writers. Mahalo Claire Calderon, Vanessa Martir & her WOL class; Connie Pertuz-Meza, M. C. Gee, Merna Dyer Skinner, Ewa Chrusciel, Deborah Krainin, Jensea Storie, Dawn McGuire, Jenny Liou; Panorama's David I. Osu & Amy Gigi Alexander; Tupelo friends, especially Kirsten Miles & D. G. Geis. Merci beaucoup to FMWG + B: Sejal Patel, Barbara Ridley, Catherine Linn, Diane Demeter, JoAnne Tompkins, Sue Granzella, Mark Nassutti, Stan Berry, Kim S. Rogers, Chivvis Moore & Blaze Farrar. Thanks to Lane Mitchell, Beth Lyon, Vicki Ferris, MAG Alumni & Friends, Kathy Scruggs, Ellen East, Laura W. Lessnau, Scott Marshall, Maria Lameiras, Lea McLees, Helen Bhattacharyya, Lance Cleland. Special love to Angie Powers, Nanou Matteson, Dorothy Hearst & Lucy Jane Bledsoe.

Thank you so much Jean Kwok, Victor LaValle, Ken Foster, Laura Juliet Wood, Kiran Desai, Julie Otsuka,

Sylvia Foley, Janet Harvey, Joanna Greenfield, Raul Correa, Andes Hruby, Jennifer Lucas, Emmy Perez, Jennifer Franklin, Desmond Barry, Molly Shapiro, Crystal Reiss, Christian Langworthy, Linne Ha, Jill Bossert, Mike & Sylvia McGregor, Tzivia Gover & most especially Amanda Gersh. Thank you CWSV Crazy 8s & Alex Espinoza, Julie Bolt & Al Young's fiction class, Colleen Morton Busch & Gill Dennis's morning crew, Annette Schiebout, Lisa Alvarez & Brett Hall Jones. Mahalo HSB family & especially Terry Luke, Cynthia Oi, Rod Ohira, Melissa Vickers, Becky Ashizawa, Greg & Norene Ambrose & especially Linda Hosek. Mahalo Bahbra Boykin & Larry Smith in Illinois, Louise Windsor & Anne V. Martino in Florida.

Thank you Kiese Laymon, Nayomi Munaweera, Shanthi Sekaran, Rajiv Mohabir, Evelyne Accad, Magda Bogin, Harry Amana, Angel Velasco Shaw, Patricia Spears Jones & especially Lucille Clifton. I am grateful for the books of Maggie Nelson, Mary Robison, Sandra Cisneros, Chitra B. Divakaruni & Claudia Rankine.

Namaste VONA poetical content family & Elmaz Abinader for bringing us together: (2015) Karineh Mahdessian, Laura G. Ramos, Tee Sarmina, Mariela Regalado, Sylvia Chavez, Damian Gonzalez, Alan Pelaez, Ramy El-Etreby, Li Ming Yu, Mackenzie MacDade, Martin Velasco Ramos, Tanzila Ahmed; & (2017) Arla S. Bull, Cinelle Barnes, Jai Dulani, John H. Joo, Nour Naas, Sarah Gonzalez, Soniya Munshi, Tina Zafreen Alam & J. Zeynab Joukhadar.

Love and gratitude to my husband & daughters & to

the Bagchi, Roychowdhury, Gupta, Chakrabarti, Dasgupta, Laskar & Sen families; A. L. & Renu Laskar, Pranab & Gauri Sen; Ru & Kim Sen, Raja & Shilpi Laskar & all of the marvelous cousins, nephews, nieces; Shankar & Ruma Sengupta, Daniella Davis, Sunanda McGarvey & family, Anjoli Roy & family, Ashmita Chatterjee & family, Korinne Lassiter, Rachael Zellner, Megan Campbell, Jenny Triplett, Kavita Rao, The Senguptas of Honolulu; Dean & Kathy Brewer, Robin Holtson, Chris Evans, Amanda Scacchitti, Beth Woodward, Susan Freiburg, Pete Apostolakis & his wonderful parents; Jay & Tanya Kruse, Jurgen & Gloria Hofler, Carolina Dourado, Walter Sorrells & Patti Hughes; & especially Faith Hoople & Luchina Fisher. Thanks Laura Wefing, Kathy McDonald, Enrique Balorya, Lori Gagnon, Frank Barbee, Becca Bradford, David McKinnis, Sherry Keen, Brad King, Sandra Grant, Pat Johnson, Christophe Neumann, Joe & Jane Render, Mrs. Gail Heath; Cindy Kuegeman & Wood Acres family; Karen Goelst, Prof. James Yee, Jill Leonard, Jay Chaudhuri & family, Rob & Pritha Roy, Sudhir Gupta & family, Eric & Helen Graben, Joyce Fitzpatrick, Jeff & Cheryl Gramling. Remembering Mrs. Kalyani Sen and J. R. & Nilima Dasgupta.

And finally, much gratitude and love to the two Elizabeths: the writer Elizabeth Rosner for her friendship, vision and gentle guiding hand; and for my "golden oldie" friend, partner in literature, the writer Elizabeth Stark for her generosity of spirit, for asking the hard questions and for listening to understand.

DEVI S. LASKAR is a native of Chapel Hill, North Carolina, and holds an MFA from Columbia University. Her work has appeared in *Tin House* and *Rattle*, among other publications. She has been nominated for a Pushcart Prize, and is an alumna of TheOpEdProject and VONA. *The Atlas of Reds and Blues* is her first novel. She lives in the San Francisco Bay Area. Find out more at devislaskar.com.